WHAT HAPPENED ON WREN HOLLOW TRAIL

Books By LG Rice

SECRETS OF SAGE MANOR SERIES
Through The Crystal Gate
Shadows Over Tanzlora
Battle For Pisgah

WHAT IF ETs ARE REAL?

GALEN VALLEY CHRONICLES
When The Past Comes Home

What Happened On Wren Hollow Trail

LG Rice

Author's Note: A Message to the Reader

While this novel is a work of fiction, it centers around themes that may be emotionally sensitive for some readers. *What Happened on Wren Hollow Trail* explores the complex and often painful topic of domestic violence. Though the events and characters are fictional, the emotional truths they represent are rooted in very real experiences faced by many.

This story follows the aftermath of a tragic shooting involving a wife and her husband, delving into the gray areas of self-defense versus murder. It is not graphic in its depiction of violence, but it does examine the emotional, legal, and societal reactions of family members, coworkers, friends, and the broader community.

My hope is that this book encourages you to think, to question, and perhaps to find ways to support or become involved with organizations that assist survivors of domestic violence. However, if this subject matter could be harmful or triggering for you in any way, please consider your well-being first. Your mental and emotional safety is paramount, and I offer this notice with care and respect.

— *LG Rice*

1

The silver bell above the Kelley Family Diner door gave its usual cheerful ring as Margaret Holloway stepped in from the sidewalk, her sensible shoes clicking softly on the polished linoleum floor. A cool gust of air met her cheeks, welcomed after the long, muggy walk down Wisteria Street. Summer had clung stubbornly to the town, but Galen Valley was finally easing into fall—or trying to.

The booths near the window already hosted their usual late-morning patrons: retirees lingering over endless cups of coffee, a young couple sharing pancakes, and Sarah Kelley herself behind the counter, flipping her notepad closed as she hollered toward the kitchen.

Margaret spotted Cassie and Kathryn at their usual table near the corner. The sun hit the plaid curtain just right, casting a warm checkered glow over Kathryn's sleek bob and oversized sunglasses resting on the table beside a cinnamon latte.

"Margaret!" Kathryn Bowen stood and gave her a quick hug. "We were just saying you'd be here any second."

Cassie Dixon grinned from behind her steaming cup of black coffee. "I said you'd time it perfectly. We haven't even ordered yet."

Margaret slid into the booth and pulled off her lightweight cardigan. "I had to stop by the library on my way. Francis left a stack of donated books on the back steps and warned me they were mostly romance paperbacks from the eighties."

Kathryn smirked. "You say that like it's a bad thing."

Cassie chuckled and set down her mug. "Let's all agree some things are best left buried."

"Like neon leg warmers and perms," Margaret added.

Laughter warmed their corner as Sarah Kelley approached, tucking her pen behind her ear. "Morning, ladies. What are we thinking?"

Kathryn leaned forward eagerly. "I'll take the autumn quiche with extra cheddar and that cranberry spritzer you're testing."

Margaret glanced at the menu out of politeness. "The pecan waffles for me, please. No syrup."

"Coffee refill, Cass?" Sarah asked.

"Please and thank you."

Sarah scribbled and walked off, hollering the order through the window to her cousin working the grill.

"I just got the new fall and winter lines in yesterday," Kathryn said, eyes sparkling. "Valley Vogue is about to look like a snow queen's closet."

"Oh?" Cassie raised a brow. "You're pivoting from pastel power suits to faux furs?"

Kathryn grinned. "Think textured neutrals with bold metallic accessories. I've got caramel wool coats, velvet flared pants, and the coziest shearling wraps. Brontë says they make me look like a luxury polar bear."

Margaret gave a half-laugh. "He's not wrong."

Brontë Sutton, the gruff, outdoorsy mountain man who had been helping out at the Sage Manor estate, had recently moved into Marshall Bowen's old hunting cabin after Marshall passed. He and Kathryn had let a simmering attraction between them grow into something more.

"I do love my mountain men," Kathryn said with a playful shrug, lifting her latte to her lips.

"After the scorcher of a summer we just had," Cassie said, "I'm ready for coats, boots, and something hot in my hands besides local government paperwork."

"Speaking of which," Margaret said, "how's the budget coming along with Russell?"

Cassie opened her mouth to answer, but the chime above the diner door rang again—this time loud and frantic.

Cassie turned just as Darlene, her assistant, burst in with hair pinned back hastily, chest heaving, cheeks flushed. She scanned the room in seconds and rushed to their table.

"Cassie—oh, thank God." Darlene gripped the edge of the table, trying to catch her breath.

Cassie stood quickly, already reaching for her purse. "What is it?"

"You forgot your phone in your office, and I didn't know where else to find you. I just got a call from Seth. It's—" She glanced at Margaret and Kathryn, who were both watching silently, concern on their faces. "It's Patrice Wallen. She was just found on the Wren Hollow Trail... kneeling beside Russell's body."

Cassie stared at her, confused. "Russell Wallen?"

Darlene nodded, eyes wide with disbelief. "She's claiming self-defense. Said he was threatening her—chasing her through the woods with a gun. There was a scuffle. The gun went off."

The booth went silent.

Margaret's hand fluttered to her chest. "Good Lord."

Kathryn dropped her fork onto her plate with a clatter. "That can't be right. Patrice? Russell? Are you sure?"

"I heard Seth's voice myself," Darlene said. "He sounded... shaken."

Cassie blinked, her mind scrambling to connect the dots. "Where exactly?"

"Pisgah National Forest. Wren Hollow Trail. Sheriff Ross is already on site."

Margaret looked to Cassie. "You worked with Russell every day. What—how could something like this happen?"

"I don't know." Cassie's voice came out thin. "He's been by my side since day one. He's the reason we dug out of the last administration's mess."

"Is," Kathryn whispered. "He is. He can't be..."

Cassie turned toward the counter and flagged down Sarah, who immediately brought her check.

"Sorry, we've got to go," Cassie said, grabbing her coat and slipping cash onto the table.

"We'll cover it," Kathryn said, standing. "Just go."

Cassie gave them a stunned, grateful nod, then turned and followed Darlene out the door, leaving behind steaming coffee, untouched food, and two shocked women in their wake.

By the time they reached Town Hall, the entire building felt like it had stopped breathing. Staff looked up from desks, paused mid-phone call, or stood talking in quiet corners. Whispers about Russell. Patrice. A gun.

Cassie pushed open the double doors to her office and immediately noticed her phone buzzing on the desk. She ignored it, dropping her purse on the chair just as her husband Seth Dixon, the District Park Ranger and Sheriff Baxter Ross walked in through the rear hallway entrance.

Seth's uniform was smudged with forest dirt. Baxter's face was carved from stone, a deep furrow between his brows.

"Seth. Baxter." Cassie stepped toward them. "Tell me what's going on."

Seth looked down for a moment before meeting her eyes. "Russell's dead, Cass. Single gunshot to the chest. Patrice was standing over him when hikers found them."

Cassie inhaled sharply. "And she said it was self-defense?"

Baxter nodded. "Says they were arguing. That he threatened her. She says he had the gun. During the struggle, it went off."

Cassie sank into the edge of her desk, bracing herself.

"I need to know—" she began, but Seth cut her off gently.

"We need access to Russell's office. Now. We have to treat it as part of the investigation. Anything—documents, files, correspondence—could be relevant."

Cassie's breath caught.

"He was... my right hand," she said, barely audible.

Seth's voice softened. "And we're going to handle this right. No matter where it leads."

Baxter cleared his throat. "We'll need to cordon off the office. Bring in the evidence team. I hope you understand."

Cassie looked up at both of them. Her face was pale, but her voice was clear.

"Do what you need to do."

2

The metallic click of the lock echoed down the corridor as Seth turned the key and pushed open the heavy wood door to Russell Wallen's office.

A sharp rush of stale air met him—dust and coffee, the scent of dry carpet and old toner. The room was dim, the blinds pulled halfway down against the late morning sun. Papers were stacked neatly on the long cherrywood desk. Russell had always been a tidy man. Precise. Intentional.

Seth took a long breath before stepping inside. Baxter followed, his boots heavier on the polished tile.

"Anything jump out at you?" Baxter asked, surveying the room.

"Not yet," Seth murmured, pulling out his phone and snapping a few photos from different angles: the desk, the shelves, the floor. Everything looked… ordinary. Like Russell would walk back in at any moment with his travel mug and budget binder, cracking some dry joke about spreadsheets.

He stepped around the desk and took more photos from behind it. A man's office always showed its real personality from the seat he lived in. There was a small wooden organizer with labeled tabs—*Receipts, Quarterlies, Grants, Town Audit*. No obvious mess, no recent files pulled out in haste. Just another workday, frozen in time.

"Drawer's locked," Seth said, testing the lower cabinet on the right. "Probably where he kept sensitive stuff."

"I'll have Darlene bring down the spare key," Baxter said, nodding toward the assistant's desk just down the hall.

Seth snapped a photo of the drawer anyway.

The room was cold in a way he couldn't quite name. It had nothing to do with temperature.

He looked up at the corkboard pinned with the town's upcoming grant cycle calendar, a few sticky notes about internal deadlines, and—oddly—a child's drawing tacked at the bottom. Crayon flowers and the word *Thanks Mr. Wallen!* in big pink letters. Seth's jaw flexed as he took a photo of that, too.

"How's the ranger station holding up?" Baxter asked, stepping closer to the windows to get a better look at the file boxes against the far wall.

"Calm for now. I've got two deputies sitting with her."

"Any statement?"

"Not officially. She was in shock. Said Russell had followed her after a fight, that he threatened her with the gun, and they struggled. That's all she's said so far. Her hands were shaking so bad she could barely hold a cup of water."

Baxter rubbed a hand across his beard. "Damn."

"I know."

They fell into silence as Seth documented the shelves, careful not to disturb anything. This was a courtesy sweep—photos, preliminary impressions. The real forensics would come when the SBI and federal teams arrived.

"How long till SBI gets here?"

"Out of Asheville. Maybe two hours," Baxter said. "Federal team's coming out of Charlotte—probably take them about four to get here."

Seth checked his watch. "Plenty of time to get everything cataloged."

A knock on the frame startled them both. They turned to see Cassie standing just outside the door, arms folded tightly across her chest.

Her eyes looked rimmed with unshed tears.

"Hey," she said, voice quiet.

Seth moved toward her, stepping into the hallway and closing the door gently behind him.

"You okay?" he asked.

"No." She gave a soft, bitter chuckle. "Where's Patrice?"

"At the ranger station. I've got her in the back room—we locked it down. Depending on how jurisdiction shakes out, she'll probably be moved to either Asheville or Charlotte. We're waiting for the teams to get here to determine next steps."

Cassie nodded, her gaze distant. "This doesn't feel real."

"I know," Seth said, his voice low and warm.

He reached out and wrapped his arms around her, pulling her into a tight embrace. She sagged against him, her forehead resting against his shoulder, her arms looping around his waist.

"I'm shocked by this," she whispered into his chest. "I thought I knew them both."

"I know, babe," he murmured, kissing the top of her head. "I know."

They stood there for a long moment in silence, the weight of what had happened pressing against them like the heavy beams of the building itself. Behind the office door, Russell's life sat frozen. Across town, Patrice's life was coming undone.

Back in the office, Baxter crouched to examine the bottom drawer of a filing cabinet, tugging gently to test resistance. When Seth returned, Baxter glanced up.

"Judge Robbins knows," he said.

Seth raised an eyebrow. "That was quick."

"Had to be. Patrice is the sitting Clerk of Court for the entire county. Her entire staff is in a tailspin right now. Court's paused indefinitely."

"What'd Robbins say?"

"He's stunned. Said he'll send a temporary administrative order by the end of the day, but he wants no part of media. Told me if reporters come knocking, he's out fishing."

Seth snorted. "That sounds like Robbins."

Baxter stood again, brushing off his hands. "He'll need to appoint a temporary acting clerk of court. Probably Amy Glaston. She's Patrice's second. Smart, steady. They'll need continuity."

"Yes, " Seth said, "that's a good call."

He stood at the desk and looked down at the chair—Russell's chair. The one Cassie used to joke was a "throne of logic." Her right hand, she'd always called him. Her fixer. Her numbers guy. The man who took her idealism and grounded it in dollars and cents.

And now?

Dead on a forest trail, a bullet through the chest, his wife claiming fear and survival.

Seth picked up a legal pad resting on the desk. The top line read:

"2026 Projected Budget Adjustments – Final Draft"

"Would he have been working on this with Cassie?"

"Almost definitely," Baxter said. "She mentioned it over lunch last week. Said he was optimistic."

Seth flipped the page. More figures. Notations in perfect block print. There was something oddly human about seeing Russell's handwriting here, just days—maybe hours—before his death. Like a ghost trying to finish the quarterlies.

"I'm going to take this pad for evidence," Seth said. "Initialing it for the record."

Baxter nodded and jotted the entry into the evidence log.

"Anything on that drawer?"

"Nope. We'll wait for the SBI team to open it officially. If Russell was hiding anything, that's where it'll be."

Seth pulled out his phone and checked the messages piling up.

Two missed calls from the DA's office. One from the forestry service. Several texts from deputies giving traffic updates about media vans starting to gather on the highway into town.

"They're circling already," he muttered.

Baxter walked toward the window and pushed the blinds aside, peeking down at the street. "They'll be at the diner, the courthouse, and Town Hall by lunch. You want me to put out a statement?"

Seth shook his head. "Not yet. Let's wait until the SBI has something official."

Baxter nodded, then let the blinds fall shut.

Outside the office, the hallway was still quiet. Seth could hear Cassie's voice down the corridor, soft, speaking to Darlene. No doubt trying to get ahead of the fallout, doing what she always did—triage, leadership, damage control. Even when her heart was breaking.

Seth looked once more around the office.

This wasn't just a crime scene. It was the epicenter of their town's political heartbeat. And now it was part of a very public—and very personal—implosion.

He rubbed his neck, fatigue setting in early.

There would be long days ahead. Statements to take. Forensics to log. Rumors to dispel. Truths to uncover.

3

The ranger station was quiet except for the hum of the overhead lights and the rhythmic creak of the chair where Deputy Justin Foster shifted his weight.

Patrice Wallen lay curled on the narrow cot in the back room—technically a holding cell, though the door remained open. She was wrapped in a green wool blanket, one issued for emergencies or cold hikers, and it smelled faintly of pine and dust.

She hadn't spoken since they brought her in.

Deputy Foster sat sideways in the door frame, one eye on her, the other on the front entrance. He was young—maybe twenty-five—with dark-blond hair under his ranger's cap and a quiet, steady way about him. He didn't fidget, didn't ask questions. He just... sat.

It was more than she could take.

Patrice had cried until her eyes stung and her throat burned. Then she'd gone quiet. Too quiet. She sat up. Lay down. Curled in a ball. Stared at the ceiling. Her body was numb except for the deep, pulsing ache in her left shoulder—the price of hitting the forest floor hard and fast.

The price of surviving.

She didn't even know what time it was.

The fluorescent lights made everything feel timeless—stuck in some awful bubble where everything real had been suspended, even sound. Even breath.

The blanket shifted as she slowly sat up again, the cot creaking beneath her. Her eyes flicked toward the door frame.

Deputy Foster noticed and gave a small nod. "Can I get you anything, Mrs. Wallen?"

She didn't answer. Couldn't.

What could she possibly say?

That she had killed her husband? That her heart still hammered with the memory of the barrel pressing into the soft skin beneath her chin? That part of her was still on that forest floor, clutching the gun, shaking, screaming *no* over and over until her voice gave out?

No. She had no words. Not yet.

She pressed her good hand to her shoulder. The skin was sore and starting to swell. She winced. A bruise would come soon. There was always a bruise. Russell made sure of it—if not on the skin, then deeper.

They'd started that morning with a hike. That's what made it all the more sickening. It was supposed to be a fresh start.

He had been told—firmly—by his doctor to improve his diet, move more, reduce stress. His blood pressure had become dangerously high. Patrice, always the helper, had started prepping fresh meals, getting him a FitBit, and even suggesting a hiking schedule. She thought it would help. That they'd connect again.

But nothing ever helped for long.

He grumbled that morning about the trail. His boots. His back. His thighs. Every step was a complaint, and she had tried—really tried—not to bite back. She reminded him gently of the doctor's warning, told him they didn't have to go far. Just a few loops. Enjoy the leaves.

That was when it happened.

One moment, they were walking. The next, he turned, face twisted with something ugly. Something dark.

And then he slapped her.

Hard.

So hard she staggered sideways and dropped the water bottle in her hand.

It hadn't happened in months. He'd been... better. Less volatile. But that morning—it was like someone flipped a switch.

She was stunned. For a heartbeat. Maybe two. And then she saw the look in his eyes.

She started running.

The fear took over like instinct. Like her bones had memorized what came after that slap. And this time, she wasn't going to wait around for it.

She ran, stumbling over rocks and roots, pushing branches from her face, her breath catching in her chest. And behind her, he cursed her name. Called her every vile word he had saved for these moments. He'd catch her. He'd "teach her a lesson."

And then he said it.

"I swear to God, Patrice, if you don't stop, I'll put a bullet in the back of your head."

She looked back—and saw the glint of the gun in his hand.

She froze.

That wasn't a threat. That was a promise.

She turned around slowly, her heart pounding like a drum in her ears. He reached her in seconds, rage twisting his features into something almost unrecognizable. He grabbed her by the arm—her bad shoulder—and flung her down like she weighed nothing.

Pain shot through her like a lightning bolt as she hit the ground, her left side catching the worst of it. She barely had time to cry out before he was on top of her, straddling her hips, shoving the barrel of the gun beneath her chin.

"You think you can run from me?" he spat, his breath hot with rage. "You ungrateful—"

She couldn't hear the rest. Her pulse roared in her ears.

Then—something inside her *snapped.*

The survival instinct took over.

She twisted her body violently, rolling to one side. He lost balance. Slid. She rolled the opposite way, kicking, scrambling. She reached for the gun—not to use it, just to get it *away* from them.

But he kept his grip. They wrestled for it, his hand over hers, both of them screaming, clawing, shoving.

Then—

BANG.

The shot ripped through the air. Everything stilled.

For a second, neither of them moved.

Then he slumped against her—heavy, limp. She gasped. Shoved him off. Rolled him onto his back.

And saw the blood.

It bloomed across his shirt, dark and wide. His eyes blinked once. Then went still.

"No…" she whispered. "No, no, no."

She pressed her hand to the wound, then snatched it away, covered in red. She grabbed the gun from the ground, dazed, her hands shaking uncontrollably.

That's when she heard the running.

Hikers. Voices. Crashing through the brush.

And when they burst through the clearing, all they saw was *her*, gun in hand, standing over the man bleeding out beneath her.

A nightmare.

A living, breathing nightmare.

Now she sat in the ranger station, wrapped in a scratchy blanket, aching in body and spirit, and still smelling like crushed leaves and gunpowder.

Deputy Foster stirred again, clearing his throat softly. "I can call for a medic if that shoulder's getting worse."

She gave the slightest shake of her head.

"I can't imagine what you're going through," he said carefully. "But I just want you to know—you're safe here."

She looked at him then, just briefly. Her eyes, glassy and red-rimmed, held a flicker of something.

Not trust. Not fear.

Something closer to *relief.*

She turned her gaze back to the floor.

For the first time in a long time, she wasn't in danger. Not from Russell. Not anymore.

And yet—her body didn't know it yet. Her nerves still fired. Her shoulders stayed hunched. Her hands trembled when she flexed them beneath the blanket.

Her soul was still curled in the woods somewhere.

But she was alive.

She was alive.

4

Cassie stood in her office at Town Hall, staring out the tall front window onto Main Street. The world looked unchanged—trees tossing gently in the wind, a woman pushing a stroller past the bakery, a cyclist weaving through parked cars.

But inside these walls, everything had shifted.

Behind her, Darlene was moving with quick, quiet precision—returning calls, forwarding messages, organizing what few press inquiries they'd already received. The town was holding its breath. But it wouldn't be long before it started to scream.

Cassie hadn't removed her coat. Her coffee sat untouched on the corner of her desk, now long cold.

Seth and Baxter had just emerged from Russell's office, both of them subdued and weary. Seth rubbed the back of his neck while Baxter gave Cassie a quick update.

"We locked it down. The SBI will do their sweep as soon as they arrive," Baxter said. "Nothing obvious, but we've flagged a drawer that was locked. No signs of struggle—place looked routine."

Cassie nodded slowly. "Thank you."

"I need to head back to the ranger station, check in on the perimeter before the state team arrives," Seth said. His eyes lingered on her face. "You sure you're okay here for a bit?"

"I'll manage," Cassie replied quietly. "Go. Just keep me posted."

Darlene stepped forward, tablet in hand, her face serious. "Before you go—fair warning."

Seth and Baxter turned toward her.

"Joyce and Lawrence Conrad are on their way here. They went to the sheriff's department first—Deputy Reese confirmed they were informed about Russell. But now... well, Joyce is demanding to see Patrice. She's insistent. Wants to confront her directly."

Seth frowned. "That's not happening."

"I know. I told Colin to stall them as long as he could," Darlene said, tapping her screen. "But they're ten minutes out. Maybe less. Insisted they see the sheriff and Deputy Reese had no choice than to tell them you were here. Sorry." She looked at Baxter with sympathy in her eyes.

Cassie pressed her fingers to her forehead. "God help us."

Joyce Wallen—now Conrad—had always been a difficult presence, with a sharp tongue and a flair for the dramatic. And Lawrence Conrad was worse in some ways: smooth, practiced, and legal-minded to the bone. His family had practiced law in Pinecrest for three generations, with partners sprinkled through Asheville and even a cousin on the North Carolina Court of Appeals.

They weren't just grieving—they were preparing for battle.

"I assume they're expecting access to evidence and procedural transparency?" Baxter asked.

Darlene nodded. "And the guarantee that Patrice doesn't escape justice."

"Damn it," Seth muttered. "They're going to blow this thing wide open before the SBI even parks their truck."

"They're not wrong to want answers," Cassie said, though her voice sounded tired even to her own ears. "Their son is dead. And their daughter-in-law is claiming it was self-defense. But... they weren't there. None of us were."

"They'll want blood, not nuance," Baxter added grimly.

Cassie nodded. "Darlene, can you keep them in the front conference room when they arrive? Offer water, coffee, a moment to breathe? Anything that buys us a few more minutes."

"I'll do my best," Darlene said, already moving for the door.

Cassie watched her go, then turned back to Seth and Baxter.

"Just—be ready," she said softly. "Joyce has claws. And Lawrence will know exactly which legal buttons to push."

Seth exhaled through his nose. "This day just keeps getting better."

He glanced toward the front doors of Town Hall, where the sun had shifted slightly, casting new shadows across the hardwood floor.

"I'm heading to the ranger station," he said, squeezing Cassie's hand as he passed. "Text me if they decide to head my way."

Cassie nodded. "I will."

Baxter gave her a parting look—quiet, steady. Then he followed Seth out, the door clicking softly behind them. Neither of them could risk talking with the Conrads about this case right now and Cassie understood that.

Five minutes later, Cassie was alone in her office when she heard Darlene's voice at the front entrance.

"Mrs. Conrad, Mr. Conrad—I understand. Please, if you'll just wait in the conference room, I'll let the mayor know you're here."

Footsteps. Heels. A walking cane striking the floor with sharp rhythm.

Then the unmistakable voice of Joyce Conrad, brittle and biting.

"Don't you dare tell me to sit down. My son is dead. *Dead.* And the woman who murdered him is sipping tea at the ranger's station? What kind of backwater circus are you all running here?"

Cassie stood and moved to the hall just as Joyce and Lawrence came into view.

Joyce looked nearly regal in her grief—dark blouse, pearls, sunglasses perched on her head despite the indoor lighting. Her face was pale, but fury sharpened every feature. Beside her, Lawrence carried himself with the quiet power of a man who knew the law and had wielded it like a sword most of his life.

"Cassie," Joyce snapped. "I want to speak with Patrice and I was told the Sheriff was here with you and only he could authorize that, so where is he?"

"That's not possible, Joyce," Cassie said gently. "The sheriff has left to meet with the state and federal authorities. Patrice is in protective custody until the investigation determines jurisdiction."

"Protective—*custody?*" Joyce barked a hollow laugh. "She should be in handcuffs!"

Lawrence stepped forward, putting a calming hand on his wife's shoulder. "We don't need a spectacle."

"Yes, we do!" Joyce shook him off. "She murdered my baby!"

Cassie's throat tightened. "Joyce, please. I'm so sorry. I truly am. I can't imagine your pain, but we have to let the investigation take its course. Right now, the State Bureau of Investigation and federal officers are en route. They'll take over from here."

Lawrence narrowed his eyes. "I hope you're securing the chain of evidence. If that gun goes missing, or paperwork is mishandled—"

"We're following every protocol," Cassie said. "Sheriff Ross and Seth are coordinating with the SBI. Everything has been documented and secured."

Lawrence gave a terse nod but didn't look convinced.

"She'll say he hit her," Joyce hissed, her voice trembling now with tears. "She'll drag his name through the mud. She'll lie. But you knew Russell, Cassie. You knew him. He was a good man. He worked beside you every day."

"I did know him," Cassie said quietly. "And I also know we owe the truth to everyone involved."

Joyce's lip trembled. Her fury was giving way to heartbreak now, cracking her veneer.

"I want justice," she whispered. "Real justice."

"You'll have it," Cassie promised, even though a chill coiled at the base of her spine. Because in cases like this—where love and violence, truth and trauma collide—*justice* often came dressed in gray.

5

Cassie gently extended her arm toward the side hallway. "Joyce, Lawrence—please. Let's sit. I'll join you."

Joyce lifted her chin, every inch of her expression tight with contempt and sorrow. Lawrence guided his wife toward the door, offering no resistance but keeping a firm hand at the small of her back.

The conference room was small, warm, and just private enough to shield them from the stir of staff on the other side of the hall. Cassie flicked the overhead lights on low and gestured toward the end of the table where three chairs were pulled out.

Joyce sat with a rigid elegance, like a woman raised never to let grief show without a fight. Lawrence remained at her side, rubbing her shoulder with a tenderness Cassie wasn't expecting from the stoic family patriarch.

"I've asked Darlene to bring coffee and water," Cassie said gently as she took the seat across from them. "Please, let me know if you need anything else."

Joyce didn't answer, her eyes fixed on a spot somewhere past Cassie's shoulder. But Lawrence gave a quiet nod of thanks.

Darlene slipped in quietly with two mugs of coffee, a bottle of water, and a box of tissues. She set them down carefully, meeting Cassie's eyes for a beat before slipping back out without a word.

For a long, strained moment, no one spoke.

Then Joyce reached for the coffee with trembling hands. She set it down just as quickly, the heat too much.

And then—she broke.

"My baby..." The whisper cracked on the word. "My son..."

Her body folded forward, grief unraveling her in waves. Sobs burst from her lips as she clutched her face, her shoulders heaving. Lawrence reached for her immediately, pulling her close, murmuring soft words Cassie couldn't hear.

Cassie sat still, letting the silence hold. There was nothing to say that would matter more than letting Joyce fall apart.

"I was supposed to go to brunch with him next week," Joyce finally choked out. "He said he'd bring Patrice—God help me—I said I'd prefer if he didn't."

Lawrence glanced toward Cassie. "We knew things were... strained in their marriage. But nothing to suggest this. Nothing violent."

Cassie kept her voice soft. "I understand. I can't imagine how devastating this is. I wanted to say... I'm deeply saddened, too. Russell wasn't just my Finance Director. He was a friend. A very good one."

Joyce wiped her eyes, still shaking.

Cassie continued, choosing her words with care. "He stood by me when I stepped into the role as mayor. Helped me make sense of the budget mess I inherited from Denise Carrow. Without him, I'm not sure we'd have stabilized things as quickly as we did. His dedication mattered. He mattered."

Lawrence gave a small nod of appreciation, rubbing Joyce's arm as she quietly cried beside him.

"He spoke highly of you, Cassie," Lawrence said. "Said you were one of the only honest ones left."

Cassie smiled faintly, a lump in her throat. "That means a great deal."

She hesitated for a moment, then added, "He and Seth went fishing just last month. Baxter joined them. They had a running contest over who could catch the biggest bass out at Shady Glen."

Lawrence gave a faint chuckle, though his eyes remained somber. Joyce didn't respond, her eyes red and unfocused.

"That's why we contacted the state and federal investigators right away," Cassie said, looking directly at Lawrence now. "Given how close Seth and Baxter were to Russell—and how important he was to all of us—we knew it was best to have outside agencies take the lead. I wanted to avoid even the hint of impropriety."

Lawrence met her gaze, nodding more firmly now. "I appreciate that professionalism. And the prudence in thinking ahead. We're not unreasonable people, Cassie. We want facts. Truth. And accountability."

"I want those things too," Cassie said. "Whatever they reveal."

Joyce straightened slowly, her tears drying now into lines of bitterness. "You'll see. She'll say he hit her. That he terrorized her. That he abused her."

Cassie didn't respond.

"She'll lie," Joyce hissed. "Just like she always does. She'll twist the story until she's the poor, pitiful victim and my son is the villain."

"Joyce..." Lawrence warned gently, but she pressed on.

"She and that scheming mother of hers—gold diggers, both of them. They never fit in with our family. They were always grasping for something more. Do you honestly think she earned her job as Clerk of Court? No. Our family name got her that position. If she'd married someone else, she'd be waiting tables, not managing legal documents."

Cassie let the silence hold.

She didn't flinch. Didn't interrupt.

But she didn't agree either.

Instead, she pivoted.

"What I can say," Cassie said calmly, "is that Russell took pride in his work here. His reports were always impeccable. He helped us prepare for audits, wrote successful grant applications, and went line by line through that disaster of a ledger we inherited from Denise Carrow. His contributions meant something to this community."

Joyce folded her arms tightly, her mouth pressed into a line.

Lawrence looked tired now—grief worn into his bones. His gaze flicked toward the window before settling back on Cassie.

"I'd like to be notified when SBI arrives," he said. "I know I won't be part of the investigation, but I'd like to know when the process officially begins."

"You'll be notified," Cassie promised.

"And if there's a hearing," Joyce added coldly, "I want to be present for every second. I want to look that woman in the eyes when she spins her little story."

Cassie rose from her chair, straightening her jacket. "I'll keep you informed as best I can. But I'd encourage both of you to try and rest today. You've had a terrible shock."

Lawrence nodded and stood, his arm sliding under Joyce's.

She looked around the room one last time like it had offended her simply by being unremarkable. "Don't let her paint him as a monster."

Cassie didn't answer.

Because truth didn't need defending from her.

It was already rising—quiet and slow—like mist over the valley. And soon, it would settle over all of them.

6

The ranger station had never seen this much activity.

Seth stood in the gravel lot, arms crossed over his chest as two black SUVs pulled up beside his unmarked truck. The vehicles bore the subtle yet unmistakable markings of the North Carolina State Bureau of Investigation—silver state seal decals, tinted windows, and just enough dust on the tires to say *we move quickly and stay awhile.*

The SUV doors opened, and the agents stepped out.

Leading the pack was Special Agent Tonya Kline, early forties, sharp gray suit, dark hair twisted into a low knot. Beside her, Special Agent Miguel Aranda, taller, broader, with sun-weathered skin and a folder already tucked under one arm. The rest of their team fanned out quickly—one agent checking comms, another already coordinating to visit the scene on Wren Hollow Trail.

"Kline. Aranda," Seth greeted with a nod. "Appreciate you making the drive from Asheville on short notice."

"Murders in national forests tend to do that," Kline replied crisply, scanning the area before her eyes landed on the station door. "She's inside?"

"She is. Patrice Wallen. Clerk of Court for Pinecrest County."

"And the weapon?"

"Recovered on-site. Secured in evidence."

Kline nodded, flipping open her folder. "We'll send a team out with a deputy ranger for scene documentation. Agent Aranda and I will begin preliminary interviews here."

Seth gestured toward the door. "Let's go inside."

The holding area was quiet when they entered. Patrice was sitting upright on the cot, arms around her knees beneath the wool blanket, her face pale but composed.

Justin sat just inside the door frame. He straightened as the agents approached.

"You did good, Foster," Seth said quietly. "Go ahead and walk the trail team out. Make sure they document the scene fully."

"Yes, sir." Justin nodded to the agents and stepped outside.

Seth turned to the lead agents. "We haven't conducted a formal interview. She gave an initial verbal claim of self-defense, but nothing beyond that."

"Then we'll proceed by the book," Aranda said, setting a portable recorder on the metal table in the corner. "Let's get her processed."

Seth stepped to the cell.

"Patrice," he said gently. "I need you to come with me."

She rose without a word, pulling the blanket around her shoulders like armor. Her face was devoid of emotion—numb, flat. Her shoulder still looked swollen, but she didn't complain.

He led her to the small office near the rear, a stark room with white walls, a single desk, and two chairs. Kline and Aranda followed, standing behind the desk as she sat down.

"Patrice Wallen," Kline began, opening a leather case. "At this time, we are placing you under arrest in connection with the shooting death of Russell Wallen. You have the right to remain silent…"

She continued through the standard Miranda warning, voice even, eyes unreadable.

"…Do you understand these rights as I've read them to you?"
Patrice nodded. "Yes."

"Do you wish to answer any questions at this time?"

"No," Patrice said. "I want a lawyer. And a phone call."

"Of course," Aranda said. He nodded toward Seth.

Seth opened the desk drawer and handed her the ranger station landline. "Take your time."

Patrice dialed slowly, pressing the receiver to her ear with her good hand. Her voice was hushed, words short and clipped. Whoever answered, it was clear from her tone that she trusted them. She gave them the basics. Told them where she was. Asked them to come.

It lasted less than two minutes.

When she hung up, she handed the receiver back wordlessly and stood. Her eyes remained on the floor.

Seth gently motioned toward the door.

"Let's head back, Patrice."

She followed without resistance.

Back in the holding area, Seth opened the cell door. She stepped inside and paused, turning to him.

"Could I get another blanket?" she asked quietly. "It's cold in here."

Seth studied her face for a moment. Her lips weren't blue, and the temperature in the room was stable, but the request didn't feel unreasonable.

Still… something tugged at his memory.

He swallowed hard. "Yeah. I'll get one."

She sat on the cot and wrapped her arms around herself again, pulling the blanket higher up her shoulders.

Seth walked down the hallway to the supply closet, his footsteps slow and heavy.

As he reached for the folded wool blankets, a flash of memory returned—unbidden and sharp.

Sheriff Marshall Bowen.

Just a few months ago, he had sat in this very holding room, pacing in tight circles after being questioned for obstruction tied to the old mayor's cover-ups. He hadn't acted despondent. Hadn't shown any of the signs. But in the early hours of morning, he had hung himself with a bed sheet in his cell.

Seth closed his eyes for a beat, the chill of it washing through him.

He took the blanket, walked back down the hall, and handed it through the bars.

"Thank you," Patrice said softly, unfolding it over her lap.

Seth lingered at the door for a second longer. She looked tired—bone deep. But not broken. Not like Marshall had looked that night.

Still, the memory was too raw.

Seth turned on his heel and walked briskly down the hallway until he reached the admin wing. Inside, his assistant, Mara Hightower, was sorting incoming correspondence and taking notes on a legal pad.

"Mara," he said. "I need you to sit just outside the holding room for a while."

She blinked, surprised. "What's going on?"

"Just observation. No interaction, no questions. I gave the suspect an extra blanket. She's not showing any red flags, but I'd rather not risk anything. You remember what happened with Marshall."

Mara's face fell. She nodded instantly. "Of course."

"Bring a tablet or your laptop. Just be present."

"I'll be there in two minutes," she said, already pulling her things together.

Seth gave her a grateful nod and returned to the main corridor, passing Agent Kline in the hallway.

"She didn't give a statement did she?" she asked.

"No," Seth replied. "Lawyer's on the way."

Kline gave a noncommittal hum. "We'll wait. We've sent a unit to the Wallen house and another to Patrice's office in Pinecrest. If there's anything to support her claim of abuse, we'll find it."

Seth nodded. "Do me a favor. Be thorough. This town can't take another scandal built on speculation."

"We always are," she said, then added more softly, "but the truth never comes easy when it's this close to home."

By late afternoon, the ranger station had shifted from quiet to buzzing.

Mara sat outside the holding room, typing steadily on her laptop with occasional glances through the bars. Inside, Patrice had wrapped herself in both blankets and lay back on the cot, eyes closed but not asleep.

The trail team returned with preliminary findings—scuff marks, signs of struggle, the approximate spot where Russell's body had landed. Blood was still drying on the forest floor.

Cassie texted Seth around 4:15 to say Joyce and Lawrence had left Town Hall but would expect updates. She asked if she should come by the station. Seth told her not yet.

Let things settle. Let the agents work. Let the process take root.

He stepped outside for a breath of fresh air, leaning against the wooden porch rail and looking toward the ridgeline, where the shadows were starting to stretch longer across the pines.

He wasn't a rookie. He knew better than to form early opinions.

But something in Patrice's eyes lingered in his mind—not guilt, not manipulation. Something quieter. Raw. Heavy.

Whatever happened out there… it had taken everything she had to survive it.

And now, the rest of them would spend the coming days piecing together a truth that had unfolded in mere seconds—on a trail meant for peace, not blood.

7

S eth stood near the door of the ranger station, arms folded as three figures stepped inside with practiced confidence and dark briefcases.

Quentin Stiles led the way—a veteran defense attorney out of Asheville, graying at the temples, impeccably dressed in a tailored navy suit. His paralegal, Emily Jacobs, followed close behind, business-casual in flats and a dark plum knit dress, clutching a tablet and a leather folder. Bringing up the rear was Abigail Wentworth, a private investigator in jeans and a fitted blazer, her expression calm but alert.

"Ranger Dixon," Quentin said by way of greeting. "We spoke earlier. We're here to see Mrs. Wallen."

"She's expecting you," Seth replied. "Follow me."

The trio walked in silence as Seth led them down the short hall toward the holding area. Patrice sat on the cot, both blankets still draped around her shoulders. She looked up the moment she heard his voice.

"Your attorney's here," Seth said gently. "We'll go back to the same room."

She nodded and stood slowly, tucking the edge of the top blanket beneath her elbow as if it helped her hold herself together.

Seth unlocked the cell door, motioned her through, and led her down the hallway to the small interview office. Quentin stepped inside, holding the door open for Emily and Abigail. Seth paused at the threshold.

"Let me know when you're finished."

Quentin nodded with crisp professionalism. "Thank you."

Then he closed the door.

"First things first," Quentin said, pulling out a few papers and a pen. "I've brought over power of attorney documentation so I can begin handling everything on your behalf—legal, financial, communications. Once you sign, I'll be authorized to speak and act for you where needed."

Patrice took the pen with unsteady fingers and signed her name in careful script. Emily clipped the pages back into a folder.

"Next," Quentin said, steepling his fingers, "I need to know what you've told anyone so far—law enforcement, the rangers, investigators."

Patrice swallowed. "I told Ranger Dixon he followed me. That he had a gun. That we fought and the gun went off. That's all."

"No mention of physical abuse? No written statements?"

She shook her head. "No. Just that. I asked for a lawyer right away after I was read my rights."

"Good," Quentin said, a touch of approval in his tone. "Then we're not dealing with any pretrial damage—yet."

He turned to Emily, who set her phone down on the table and opened a voice memo app.

"Let's get this recorded while it's fresh," she said. "Only for internal purposes. This isn't a statement to authorities."

Abigail leaned forward slightly. "We're all here to help you, Patrice. Just take your time."

Patrice nodded and stared at the table, gathering herself.

Then—slowly—she began.

She described the start of their morning. The hike. The doctor's orders. The suddenness of the slap. The look in Russell's eyes.

She told them about running—about how the slap felt like a warning shot to something far worse. How the fear had screamed in her ears before he even said a word.

Then came the gun.

His threat.

His hands.

The weight of him pressing her into the ground, the cold steel beneath her chin.

The struggle.

The shot.

His body slumping over hers like a cut rope.

The shock. The horror. The disbelief as the blood spread across his chest.

She spoke in starts and stops, sometimes stammering, sometimes silent. At times, her voice was no more than a whisper.

By the end, her hands were trembling.

Tears fell freely down her cheeks. She didn't wipe them away.

Abigail reached out, gently covering Patrice's hand with her own.

She assured her that she'd be thorough in her investigation, planned to compile a detailed list of questions, and said they'd be meeting again soon—either once she was transferred to the detention center in Asheville or, hopefully, released on bail.

Patrice didn't respond. Just looked down at her hands.

Quentin leaned forward, nodding at Emily to stop the recording.

"We'll need to gather every photo, every medical record. If he ever sent texts—voicemails—that'll matter. We'll start building this now. But I want you to know, Patrice—your story is clear. It's painful. And it matters."

Patrice looked at him, eyes hollow.

"I didn't mean to kill him."

"I believe you," Quentin said. "But we'll still have to prove it."

He stood, smoothing the front of his jacket. "Get some rest. I'll coordinate with the SBI and the courts. We'll figure out next steps."

Patrice nodded faintly.

Seth was waiting outside when Quentin stepped out, and silently returned Patrice to her cell. She walked more slowly this time, with the heavy exhaustion of someone who had unburdened too much.

Once she was settled inside, Seth turned to Mara Hightower again. "Stay with her, please. She's stable, but I don't want her alone."

"Got it," Mara said, sliding her chair back toward the holding room.

Outside in the main hallway, Quentin and his team gathered their things. Agent Tonya Kline approached them with a tablet in one hand and a half-finished coffee in the other.

"You're finished with the client?" she asked briskly.

Quentin nodded. "For now. I'll be back in the morning, but I'd like to request she be transferred to the detention center in Asheville. If a bail hearing is possible, it's better she be there in preparation."

Kline raised an eyebrow and actually chuckled. "You're welcome to prepare, Mr. Stiles, but I highly doubt any judge in the state will grant her release. She's being charged with first-degree murder, and it happened on federal land."

"I'm aware," Quentin replied coolly. "But a request for transfer to a more secure facility still stands."

Kline sipped her coffee. "We feel a more secure location is appropriate, too. Asheville is fine with us."

"Thank you," he said with a sharp nod, then turned to Emily and Abigail. "Let's go."

As the trio exited the station, Kline watched them disappear through the glass doors and shook her head.

"Stiles is good," she muttered. "But he's crazy if he thinks any judge will set bail on this. I don't care if she's the Pinecrest County Clerk of Court or the Queen of England."

Seth leaned against the doorframe. "They'll fight like hell. That team's no joke."

"No, they're not," Kline said. "Which means we'd better make damn sure we do everything by the book. I don't want this case unraveled on a technicality because someone forgot to initial an evidence label."

Seth nodded slowly. "Agreed."

He glanced back down the hall toward the holding room where Patrice sat—behind bars but still gripping something that looked an awful lot like hope.

Whatever the next move was, it would be a hard one.

Because in Galen Valley, the truth never stayed buried for long.

8

The scent of grilled burgers and hot dogs drifted lazily over the back porch of the Dixon house, curling into the cool night air. Cicadas buzzed in the distance, and the occasional pop of the grill punctuated the silence that hung heavy between the four chairs arranged in a circle around the patio firepit.

Cassie sat on the porch swing, legs tucked under her, holding a mason jar of sweet tea with both hands. Her eyes were glassy from fatigue, her lipstick long faded. Seth stood near the grill, flipping patties with a slow deliberation that had more to do with distraction than dinner.

Baxter leaned back in his Adirondack chair, beer resting against his knee, while Natalie sat beside him, freshly returned from her trip up north.

Cassie had hugged her tight when she'd arrived, despite the shadow of Russell's death hanging over them all. She'd missed her friend—and tonight, she needed her more than she realized.

"So?" Cassie asked, nudging Natalie's leg with her foot. "You're back from New York and full of secrets. Spill. Was it a mob boss? A scandal involving overpriced yoga retreats?"

Natalie grinned, taking a sip of her water. "Nice try."

"Oh, come on," Cassie pleaded. "Give me *something*. Even a cryptic quote or hint."

"Nope." Natalie's voice was light, but her expression didn't waver. "It's still embargoed. I signed three NDAs and had to turn my phone off for twelve hours straight."

Cassie groaned. "You're killing me."

Seth chuckled softly. "She's been pestering you all night."

"It's the only fun thing we've got going, and she won't let me have it!" Cassie mock-pouted before her tone softened. "But I am glad you're back. Today's been… a mess."

Natalie nodded, her smile fading. "I heard the news before my plane even landed."

Baxter exhaled deeply and ran a hand over his jaw. "It's hard to believe. Russell Wallen. Shot. Patrice in custody."

Seth carried a tray of burgers and buns over to the patio table and sat down with a tired sigh. "It still doesn't feel real."

Cassie shook her head. "No, it doesn't."

"She made biscuits," Baxter said suddenly. "Patrice. A few times, when we picked Russell up for early morning fishing. She'd pack them in foil, hot and buttery. One time she even tucked a jar of homemade jam in the cooler."

Seth nodded. "Yeah. I remember that. She wasn't just… civil. She was kind. Quiet, sure. A little withdrawn. But never rude. Never cold."

"She always seemed polite to me too," Natalie added. "Which makes all of this harder to process."

"It's a strange thing," Baxter said, his eyes distant. "I can't say that I don't believe her story."

Seth met his gaze. "Same."

Natalie blinked. "Really?"

Seth leaned forward, elbows on his knees. "Nothing we saw out on that trail contradicts her version of events. There were signs of a scuffle. One shot. No second weapon. And the bruising on her arm—looks fresh, like it happened during a physical altercation."

"But," Baxter added, "she was standing over his body with the gun in her hand when the hikers found her. That's going to be hard for Stiles to get past in court. It looks bad. Even if it *isn't* what it seems."

Cassie nodded solemnly. "And Joyce Conrad... well. If you could have heard her this afternoon—she's already got Patrice tried, convicted, and marching to the gas chamber."

"She that bad?" Natalie asked.

"She's lethal about it," Cassie replied. "No space for doubt. No desire to see beyond her version of Russell."

"She's grieving," Natalie offered gently.

"She's grieving and launching a crusade," Cassie said. "And she's not alone. Lawrence was measured, but he's just as determined. I guarantee they'll push for the death penalty. They've already hinted at it."

Silence fell again, broken only by the crickets and the soft clink of ice in Natalie's glass.

"This is a heartbreaking situation all the way around," Natalie finally said. "No matter which way it goes. A man is dead. A woman is shattered. And a town is going to have to find its moral compass while watching it all unfold in the spotlight."

"Yep," Baxter agreed. "And no one wants to talk about what happens if the courts believe her. What that means for his legacy. His family."

"Or what it means," Seth added, "if they don't believe her—and she really was just trying to survive."

Cassie looked up at the stars, blinking back the sting in her eyes. "This is going to divide people. I can feel it."

"It already is," Baxter said.

"And the media hasn't even descended yet," Natalie said. "But they will. It's coming."

Cassie sighed. "Let them come. We'll do what we've always done—face it, deal with it, and try to protect Galen Valley in the process."

Seth reached over and took her hand, squeezing it gently.

"I just hope the truth makes it out of this intact," Cassie added softly.

Natalie raised her glass slightly. "To truth."

They all echoed the word—quietly, solemnly—as smoke drifted up from the dying embers in the grill and the night deepened around them.

The world beyond their small circle was shifting. But for this one moment, in the stillness of a Galen Valley evening, they were simply four friends—trying to make sense of it all.

9

Abigail climbed the worn stone steps of the Pinecrest County Courthouse, the weight of Quentin's instructions pressing against her spine like a loaded briefcase. The town was buzzing with speculation, and she was hoping—perhaps foolishly—that the state and federal teams hadn't yet made it to Patrice's office.

The building's interior was hushed, almost reverent, and the scent of old paper and fresh coffee hung in the air. She made her way to the clerk's wing, the heels of her boots clicking across the polished floor. Stopping at the reception window, she leaned in slightly toward a younger woman wearing a gold nameplate that read *Winnie*.

"Hi," Abigail said with a polite smile. "I'm working with Patrice Wallen's legal team, and I was hoping to retrieve a few personal items from her office that she has requested. Can someone assist me?"

Winnie's eyes widened with visible discomfort. "Oh… I'm sorry, but you'll need to speak with one of the deputies about that."

Abigail tilted her head. "Is the office secured?"

"Yes, ma'am," Winnie replied. "It's been locked by order of the District Attorney. We were told no one is allowed access to Clerk Wallen's workspace until further notice—direct instruction from Tabitha Welsh."

Abigail's jaw tightened as she exhaled slowly, masking her irritation. So the DA had gotten here first after all.

"Who would I need to speak with?" she asked calmly.

"Deputy Mendez is on rotation today," Winnie offered, glancing toward the hallway that led to the courthouse security office. "He can give you more information. But I was told it's completely off-limits, even for staff."

Abigail nodded once. "Thank you."

She walked away from the clerk's suite, her heels tapping a steady rhythm as she made her way down the long corridor to the courthouse security office. She'd expected resistance—but not this soon, not like this. Still, she wasn't about to leave without at least making an official attempt.

The door to the security office was slightly ajar. She knocked once, then stepped in.

Deputy Mendez, a thick-set man in his forties with salt-and-pepper stubble and tired eyes, looked up from behind the counter.

"Can I help you?" he asked, voice brusque and already impatient.

Abigail offered her most professional expression. "Yes, I'm Abigail Wentworth. I'm a licensed private investigator working with Patrice Wallen's legal team. I'd like access to her office to retrieve some personal items at the request of her attorney."

Mendez's face didn't budge. "No can do."

"I'm not asking for anything confidential," Abigail said evenly. "Just to check her desk. Anything personal—photographs, letters, things of that nature."

"It's been locked," Mendez said. "District Attorney Welsh ordered it sealed until further notice."

Abigail remained calm. "I understand that. But again, I'm not with the press or the public. I'm working on behalf of her counsel. If you just let me retrieve her personal—"

"I'm aware of who you are," he cut in. "And I'm also aware you could get access with a subpoena. But you don't have one right now. So until that changes, you're not going in. Not today."

Abigail inhaled slowly, resisting the urge to bite back. Instead, she smiled—the kind of smile that held no warmth at all.

"Fine. Understood," she said. "I'll be back—with a subpoena. And next time, I'll have authority to go through everything."

Mendez raised a brow, unimpressed. "Looking forward to it."

She gave a nod, turned on her heel, and strode out of the security office, her exit just as composed as her entrance. Her tone, as she passed back through the lobby? Sarcastic.

"Have a nice day," she drawled.

And she didn't mean a word of it.

Abigail had barely shut the door of her car before she pulled out her phone, tapped Quentin's name, and brought it to her ear with a sigh. The courthouse windows glinted behind her like smug sentinels. She didn't even bother starting the engine.

Quentin picked up on the second ring. "Tell me you got something."

"Nope," Abigail said, irritation simmering beneath her calm tone. "Security's locked down Patrice's office tight—under direct order from Tabitha Welsh. Deputy Mendez practically laughed in my face. Said I'm welcome to come back with a subpoena."

"Of course," Quentin muttered. "She's already marking her territory."

Abigail leaned her head back against the headrest. "So what now? Do we go through the trouble of filing for the subpoena, or just wait on discovery?"

There was a brief pause. Then Quentin said, "According to Patrice, the only thing in her desk was a notebook with a few entries. Nothing she thought would help us much. The real gold is in her journals—the ones taken from the house. I've already submitted a formal request to review those through discovery."

Abigail nodded, shifting gears in her head. "Got it. So then what's my next move?"

"Come on back to the office," Quentin said. "Let's regroup and figure out the next step from there."

"Copy that," she replied. "On my way."

She hung up, slid the phone onto the passenger seat, and finally started the car. As the engine hummed to life, she threw one last look at the courthouse in her rearview mirror.

This wasn't over—not even close.

And next time, she'd be back with more than just a polite smile.

10

Cassie Dixon stood in front of the mirror in her office, smoothing the lapels of her navy blazer and adjusting the silver pin she'd clipped above her heart—a small magnolia bloom, carved delicately from mother-of-pearl.

It had belonged to her grandmother.

She wore it when strength needed to look like grace.

Behind her, Darlene moved efficiently through the morning routine—setting out folders, confirming the town council attendance roster, and handing Cassie a fresh mug of coffee without needing to ask.

"How are we doing?" Cassie asked, still looking at her reflection.

"Nervous," Darlene said honestly, glancing at the agenda on her clipboard. "No one wants to appear insensitive, but the town budget doesn't pause for mourning."

Cassie sighed and turned from the mirror. "I know. And Russell wouldn't have wanted it to. He hated inefficiency."

Darlene smiled faintly. "He did."

Cassie moved to her desk and opened the manila folder holding notes for the afternoon's public statement and the council meeting. There was no easy way to do this. Russell's death was still a fresh, jagged wound—and she was about to step into a room full of people trying to pretend it was business as usual.

But Galen Valley needed direction.

And she was the one expected to give it.

An hour later, the council chambers buzzed with murmurs and subdued greetings as members filed into their seats. The usual chatter about potholes and planning permits was gone, replaced by somber expressions and the occasional handshake of condolence.

Cassie stood at the head of the long table, her notes in front of her, hands lightly clasped as she waited for everyone to settle.

Once they did, she looked up and began.

"Thank you all for coming on such short notice. I know we're here under incredibly difficult circumstances."

She paused.

"As you all know, Galen Valley suffered a tremendous loss this past weekend. Russell Wallen was more than our Finance Director. He was a fixture of this community—a pillar of integrity who served under multiple administrations, including one that threatened to dismantle everything this town stood for."

A few heads nodded solemnly.

Cassie continued, "He kept records that helped convict former Mayor Denise Carrow—records that he protected and preserved at personal and professional risk. Because of that courage, this town was able to rebuild."

She exhaled, her voice dipping lower. "I knew Russell. We all did. He wasn't just a co-worker or a department head. He was a friend. A confidant. A man who showed up early and stayed late and never once asked for recognition. And now, we are all left to grieve his sudden and tragic passing."

No one interrupted. The silence in the room was reverent.

"That said," Cassie added gently, "his role in town government cannot remain vacant. Our fiscal reports, our grant submissions, our end-of-year audits—all are on tight timelines, and we must be diligent in keeping Galen Valley moving forward."

A few council members glanced down at their papers.

"I want to be very clear—we are not rushing to replace him. We are acknowledging that the work he did was critical and ongoing, and it must be continued. Out of respect for his legacy, we must do this thoughtfully."

There were a few murmurs of agreement.

Cassie continued, "We'll issue a temporary appointment to cover the immediate tasks while we prepare a formal search. I've spoken with the deputy finance officer, Angela Wilkes, and she's agreed to step in short term. She worked closely with Russell and is the most knowledgeable person available to ensure continuity."

"She's a solid choice," Councilman Eli Graves said. "Quiet, but efficient."

"And well-liked," added Councilwoman Donna Tran. "People trust her."

Cassie nodded. "Exactly. But I also want to make it clear—we're going to give the town time to grieve. We will not begin interviews or public posting for a permanent replacement until after the memorial services have taken place."

The council nodded in agreement, their expressions heavy but resolute.

Cassie leaned into the table slightly. "We are walking a fine line between moving forward and honoring the loss. But I trust us to do it with grace and respect."

Later that afternoon, Cassie stood on the steps of Town Hall, cameras trained on her, as she delivered her official public statement.

Darlene stood off to the side with a small press team and members of the town council, offering quiet support.

Cassie cleared her throat, took a breath, and began.

"Today, we mourn the loss of Russell Wallen—not just as Finance Director for the town of Galen Valley, but as a friend, a colleague, a son, and a deeply committed member of our community."

Her voice rang clearly through the small crowd gathered on the lawn and along the sidewalk.

"Russell's work behind the scenes was vital to the progress we've made as a town over the past several years. He was instrumental in helping us recover after the previous administration's mismanagement, and he gave his time and his talent freely to ensure we would not only survive—but thrive."

She paused, then continued.

"This is a time of grief. It is also a time when we must be cautious with our words, our judgments, and our assumptions. There are many things still unknown, and I urge all of us—residents, reporters, and representatives—to let the investigation unfold thoroughly and impartially."

She scanned the crowd, meeting eyes where she could.

"Rumors and speculation do not serve us. But unity does. Compassion does. Let us come together as neighbors, as friends, as a town that has weathered loss before and will weather this, too. Let us support the Wallen family with our presence, our kindness, and our prayers."

Cassie looked down briefly at her final note, then returned to the crowd with a steady voice.

"We have suffered a tragic event. But we are Galen Valley. And we will rise—together."

A soft wave of applause followed her final words—not loud, not performative. Just heartfelt.

The crowd lingered a moment longer. Conversations resumed in hushed tones. Reporters began taking notes and murmuring into their phones. And above it all, the late afternoon sun filtered through the turning leaves like a quiet blessing.

Cassie stepped down from the podium and moved to rejoin Darlene.

The words were spoken.

Now, the healing—and the reckoning—would begin.

11

Cassie Dixon sat at her kitchen table with her laptop open, a mug of tea going cold beside her, and a tightening in her chest that no amount of chamomile could touch.

The screen in front of her glowed with headlines, comments, re-posts, and a growing web of speculation. It had only been twenty-four hours since her public plea for calm, reason, and restraint—but online, that grace period had come and gone.

The townspeople were posting.

And they were not holding back.

It started with a single post:

"Cousin of my best friend was on the trail that day. Said she heard Patrice say, 'I'm glad I killed you, you abusive jerk,' while standing over his body. Gun still smoking."

It wasn't verified. It didn't come from any official statement. But that didn't stop it from being reposted over three hundred times in a matter of hours.

Then came the second claim:

"Someone close to law enforcement told me she didn't just shoot him once—she unloaded on him. Multiple shots to 'make sure he was dead.'"

Cassie rubbed her temples, frustration building behind her eyes. Neither story matched the forensic evidence so far. One gunshot. One entry wound. And no such statement had been reported by the hikers who found Patrice.

But logic didn't matter.

Not online.

Within hours, the vilification of Patrice Wallen was in full swing.

Instagram story screenshots showed people accusing her of "hunting her husband like prey." TikTok videos with ominous music claimed she had "finally snapped" after years of pretending to be the quiet, dutiful wife.

The comments were worse:

"She always looked off to me. Too quiet. Too cold."

"Makes you wonder how she landed Russell in the first place."

"I bet she poisoned his food, too. Just took it up a notch this time."

And then Joyce Conrad found the hashtags.

Cassie had been waiting for it, dreading it, knowing that Russell's mother—formidable, grief-stricken, and laser-focused—would not sit quietly in the wings.

Joyce began commenting on posts. Then she started making her own.

Her first message came in the form of a blunt Facebook post:

"Let me tell you something about Patrice Austin Wallen. She never cooked for my son. Never folded his clothes. Let their house go to ruin. And now she wants people to believe SHE was the victim? Please. She never loved him. And now she's killed him."

Within twenty minutes, it had over 500 shares.

Cassie's phone buzzed with texts from town staff asking what to say. News stations started calling Darlene's office again. A local podcast even asked for an interview "from a leadership perspective" on how to handle suspected female murderers in positions of public trust.

Cassie closed the laptop and leaned back, heart heavy.

So much for coming together.

Meanwhile, in Quentin's law office, the blinds were drawn low against the afternoon sun. The light that filtered in cast long slants across the conference table, where Abigail, Emily, and Quentin sat in tight formation. The room was quiet, heavy with anticipation.

Abigail perched on the edge of her chair and said, "Ok, let's see what she documented."

Patrice's journals had recently been turned over by Tabitha Welsh as part of preliminary discovery. They'd come from the home search, and this was the first chance the defense team had to dig into them.

Quentin slid the first one out, flipping it open. Emily and Abigail did the same.

Minutes passed in silence as pages turned. The air grew still.

"She didn't write much about the abuse," Abigail finally said, frowning. "Not the kind of detail I was expecting."

Emily nodded. "Mostly feelings about the marriage. Lots of sadness. Isolation. But no blow-by-blow."

"She wasn't trying to build a paper trail," Abigail said. "She was just surviving."

Quentin didn't speak. He flipped through another journal, expression unreadable. Eventually, he closed the book and set it down.

"I'm filing a motion to change the venue."

Both women looked up at once.

"Really?" Emily asked.

"She's too well-known here," Quentin said. "Between the court staff, her role in the community, and the press coverage… Pinecrest County is the wrong place to hold this trial. She deserves neutrality. I'll ask that it be moved to Buncombe County, and I'll request a superior court judge from the eastern part of the state—someone who doesn't know her, or the Conrads."

"Do you think Tabitha will fight you on it?" Abigail asked.

"She shouldn't," Quentin said. "If she wants a conviction that sticks, she won't risk a mistrial based on bias."

He reached for his notepad and scribbled a reminder.

"Emily—make sure I call Tabitha first thing in the morning. We'll need to discuss the change of venue before I file anything formal."

"Got it," she said.

The room fell into quiet again, the journals casting long shadows across the table. The weight of the truth wasn't easy—but they were ready to carry it into court.

Back in Galen Valley, Cassie's porch light flicked on as she stepped out onto her front stoop, phone in hand, skimming the latest post.

"If I were Russell's ghost, I'd haunt that woman 'til the day she dies."

She clicked the comment section—regretting it the moment she did.

"She'll walk free like all the rest. We never get justice anymore."

"Joyce should sue the state for hiring her."

"Bet the mayor's covering for her, too. She and Russell were close. Too close?"

Cassie turned off her phone and shoved it into her coat pocket.

It had only just begun.

And if truth had any hope of surviving in Galen Valley, they'd all need to push through a storm of half-truths, hurt, and hashtags to find it.

12

The bell above the Kelley Family Diner gave a cheerful chime as Cassie stepped inside, the warm scent of coffee and cinnamon rolls wrapping around her like a familiar shawl. The booths along the windows were already occupied by the regulars, and Sarah Kelley gave a wave from behind the counter as she slid a plate of biscuits and gravy to a man with the day's newspaper folded in front of him.

Cassie spotted Kathryn and Margaret already in their usual corner booth—Kathryn thumbing through a style magazine while Margaret sipped her tea with a faraway look in her eyes. Natalie arrived right behind Cassie.

"Well, if it isn't the full breakfast brigade," Natalie said as she shrugged out of her scarf.

"Finally, something normal," Kathryn said, pushing the magazine aside and sliding into storytelling mode. "Although, I'm not sure anything's truly normal anymore."

Cassie settled into the booth beside Margaret. "It's not. Have you seen the comments online lately? I know I said what I said in the press statement, but I don't think anyone's listening."

"Listening?" Kathryn snorted softly. "They've already formed their own court and handed down their verdict—with memes, no less."

"It's vicious," Natalie agreed. "They're not just blaming Patrice. They're tearing her life apart. Picking through rumors, gossip, twisting stories. It's character assassination in bite-sized posts."

Margaret set her teacup down gently. "I feel blessed, truly, that I grew up in a world with no internet and only three television channels. When something terrible happened, we processed it around a dinner table, not across a thousand comment threads."

Kathryn gave a slow nod. "Same here. You had one paper, a couple of radio stations, and actual conversations. Now? One person says something half-cooked online and suddenly it's gospel."

"Social media's a double-edged sword," Cassie said, stirring her coffee slowly. "It can raise awareness, spread hope, connect people—but when it's used to wound, it's relentless."

Natalie leaned forward. "I've seen stories warped into fantasy within hours. And the damage it does—it's not just emotional. It taints juries. Alters public perception. Once you become the villain of the week online, it's nearly impossible to claw your way back."

Their breakfasts arrived—scrambled eggs and toast for Natalie, a ham and cheese omelet for Cassie, pancakes for Margaret, and Kathryn's yogurt parfait with granola. The conversation slowed as forks scraped plates and coffee cups were refilled.

As they finished their meal and started bundling into coats and scarves, Cassie thanked Sarah at the register while the others gathered near the front door.

Margaret paused and turned to Cassie, touching her elbow lightly. "Can I talk to you for a minute?"

"Of course," Cassie said, stepping back from the group.

They moved to the side of the diner's entryway, near the old coat rack and bulletin board lined with flyers for bake sales and lost pets.

Margaret's eyes softened with a kind of hesitant sorrow. "I wasn't sure if I should bring this up, but... I feel like I'd be wrong not to."

Cassie nodded gently. "Go ahead."

"Patrice was in my English class when she was in high school. Quiet, thoughtful, a solid writer. Five years ago, I ran into her at the mall in Asheville. We were both shopping—random timing—and she suggested we get lunch."

Cassie's eyebrows lifted. "I didn't know you kept in touch."

"We didn't," Margaret said. "That was the first time I'd seen her in years. But she asked me something at that lunch… something that's been coming back to me ever since I heard what happened."

Cassie tilted her head. "What was it?"

"She asked me—very casually—what I would do if I were in an abusive marriage… but felt like I couldn't leave because my husband had threatened to hunt me down and kill me."

Cassie's breath caught.

"She framed it like it was a legal case," Margaret added quickly. "Said it was something coming through the court—this woman who poisoned her abusive husband and was now on trial for murder. Claimed it was self-defense, but she'd been convicted anyway."

"What did you tell her?" Cassie asked softly.

"I said I would hope I'd have a friend or family member I could trust. Someone to help me escape the situation before it turned deadly. And I said I prayed the woman had a chance at appeal. Patrice nodded along… agreed. But when we parted ways, I had this strange feeling she hadn't asked me about a case at all."

Cassie didn't answer right away. She studied Margaret's face, seeing the weight of what she was sharing.

"I always meant to reach back out," Margaret said, her voice smaller now. "Just a lunch. A check-in. Something. But life happened and I let it go."

"You couldn't have known, Margaret."

"I know. But I still wonder… if she was trying to tell me something in a roundabout way."

Cassie touched her hand. "We all wonder things in hindsight. But no one could've seen this coming."

Margaret nodded slowly, then hesitated again. "Do you know if they allow visitors at the jail in Pinecrest?"

Cassie's expression shifted. "She's not there. They moved her to Asheville after she was denied bail. It keeps her closer to Quentin Stiles' office."

"Oh."

"If you're thinking about visiting her," Cassie said carefully, "you'd need to go through Quentin. But, Margaret... I really don't recommend it. The attention on this case is growing by the hour. All it would take is one person snapping a photo of you entering that jail to start a whole new storm. Your name would be everywhere."

Margaret's shoulders dropped with a sigh. "Good point."

"I know your heart's in the right place," Cassie added gently. "But sometimes protecting ourselves means staying one step back."

Margaret gave a reluctant nod. "You're right."

They stepped outside to join the others on the sidewalk, the air crisp with late autumn chill. Natalie and Kathryn were chatting about weekend plans, trying to reclaim some normalcy amid the chaos.

As they walked away from the diner, Cassie felt the weight of Margaret's story pressing quietly on her chest.

Patrice had tried to ask for help—in her own way.

And now the question lingered like morning fog:

Had anyone truly been listening?

13

The blinds in Quentin Stiles' office were drawn against the late morning sun, casting the room in a soft, contemplative shadow. Abigail Wentworth sat near the window with her tablet in her lap, fingers poised over the keyboard. Emily Jacobs prepared the digital recorder on the table. Quentin stood near the file cabinet, flipping through case notes, glancing up as the door opened.

Valerie Austin stepped inside, her purse clutched tightly in both hands.

She was a slight woman, early sixties, with dark brown eyes and a face that bore the marks of a hard-lived life. She looked as though she had aged considerably in the past week. Her mouth was drawn in a tight line—not from bitterness, but restraint.

"Thank you for coming in, Ms. Austin," Quentin said, gesturing toward the empty chair across from him. "We appreciate your time."

Valerie sat slowly, placing her purse on the floor beside her. "I told Patrice I would cooperate in any way I could."

"We're hoping to understand more about what may have happened in her marriage to Russell," he said. "We won't show you anything or tell you anything that might color your answers—we're just going to ask a few questions."

Valerie nodded. "I'll tell you what I can."

Quentin sat across from her, his voice steady. "Did you ever witness, directly or indirectly, signs that your daughter was in an abusive relationship?"

Valerie blinked slowly, looking down at her hands. "At first, no. When they got married, she seemed happy. I thought she'd done

55

well—marrying into the Conrad family, stability, prestige. I mean, that's what any mother wants, right? Someone who'll take care of her daughter."

Abigail said nothing, letting the silence stretch long enough for honesty to fill the space.

"But then…" Valerie cleared her throat. "Over time, she stopped visiting as often. Calls got shorter. She used to come by for dinner every other Sunday. That changed. One time she came and barely touched her food. I noticed her wrist was swollen—she claimed she fell while gardening."

"And you didn't believe her?" Emily asked gently.

"I did… and I didn't." Valerie's eyes welled slightly. "She's always been strong. Private. I didn't want to insult her by pushing. But there were moments. A bruise on her collarbone. A faint cut on her lip. She always had an explanation, and I—"

She stopped, voice cracking.

"You wanted to believe her," Quentin finished.

Valerie nodded. "Yes."

"Did she ever *tell* you that Russell was hurting her?"

"No. Not in so many words. But one day about two years ago, she showed up unannounced. Just… walked in my house. Eyes red, nose running. Said she needed a shower and to sleep on my couch. I asked if she and Russell had fought, and she just looked at me and said, 'It was my fault. I should have kept my mouth shut.' That's when I knew."

Quentin leaned forward. "Thank you. That's very helpful."

When Valerie left a few minutes later, Quentin turned to Abigail and Emily.

"She knew," he said. "And she was scared, just like Patrice was."

That afternoon, Quentin made the call to the specialist in Charlotte.

Dr. Sophia Molina arrived the next morning in a gray wool coat, glasses tucked low on her nose, and a small leather briefcase in hand.

She was a licensed trauma counselor and court-certified expert in domestic abuse dynamics. Her testimony had helped shape verdicts in three counties. Her reputation preceded her.

Quentin greeted her at the entrance to the detention center in Asheville and escorted her through to the secure counseling room. A guard unlocked the door, and Patrice Wallen looked up from the small wooden table as the woman entered.

"Patrice," Quentin said gently. "This is Dr. Sophia Molina. I am going to step outside and let you ladies talk."

Patrice gave a faint nod. Her shoulders were stiff, eyes wary.

Sophia offered a warm smile as she sat across from her, setting her case on the floor.

"I'm here as a counselor," she said, voice soft but direct. "I'm not here to interrogate or challenge you. I've been asked to evaluate your state of mind and listen to anything you're willing to share."

Patrice gave a tired nod. "Okay."

The session began slowly. Dr. Molina asked about her childhood, her college years, how she and Russell met. Her tone was conversational—never pressing too hard, but never dancing around the tension in the air.

Patrice answered in short, careful sentences. She described the way Russell charmed her and her mother. How Lawrence Conrad helped her get her first job as a clerk at the courthouse before the wedding. How she started shrinking little by little until she barely recognized herself.

An hour passed before the shift happened.

Dr. Molina leaned forward, her voice barely above a whisper.

"Did you ever go to the hospital, Patrice?"

That was the breaking point.

Patrice crumpled, a sound escaping her lips that was somewhere between a sob and a laugh. "Yes," she whispered. "Twice. Two summers ago."

Sophia said nothing. Just waited.

"He beat me in the face. Said I embarrassed him at a barbecue by correcting him in front of his friends. The first time, I told the doctors I fell down the stairs. The second time… they took pictures. Said they were documenting it. Wanted me to press charges."

"But you didn't."

"I told them I'd sue if they used his name. I said they didn't know who his stepfather was. I said it was a misunderstanding. And I left."

Sophia stayed silent, letting Patrice unravel.

"I was afraid of him. Afraid of losing everything. And now he's gone, and I'm sitting here being made into the villain. But I'm not. I'm not."

She looked up, eyes fierce through the tears. "I will sign whatever you need. I will give you permission to get those records and make those doctors testify. I'm not going to prison for defending myself against an abusive monster."

Sophia reached out and touched her hand gently. "Are you sure you want to fight this fight, Patrice? The Conrad name carries weight in legal circles. They have power, connections—across the state."

"I don't care," Patrice said.

Her voice was flat. Certain.

"He was a monster. I want the world to know. I stayed too long, I know that. I made excuses, told myself it would get better. But I'm done feeling ashamed for what I endured. I don't feel weak anymore."

She wiped her tears with the back of her hand.

"I'm sorry he's dead. I really am. I loved him. I wanted him to change. But he didn't. He *enjoyed* hurting me. He *liked* controlling me. And now that I've had time to sit with it, to think about everything—"

Her eyes burned with a new kind of clarity.

"I need to fight. Not just for me—but for every woman sitting in a house right now, trying to hide the bruises. Even if they convict me, even if I spend the rest of my life in prison… I'll bring awareness to this in that courtroom."

She drew a long breath, steady now.

"I am not guilty of first-degree murder. I am guilty of killing my husband in a struggle for my life. If the court wants to convict me for that, fine. But that is the truth."

Dr. Molina nodded. "Then let's make sure it's heard."

She stood, gathered her things, and left the room with her briefcase in hand—carrying more than just documents now.

She carried evidence of truth.

14

Cassie was halfway through her second cup of coffee and deep in a spreadsheet on economic development grants when a soft knock sounded at her office door.

She looked up to find Angela, the town's acting finance director, standing in the doorway holding a thick manila folder, her brow furrowed and her eyes serious.

"Got a minute?" Angela asked.

"Of course." Cassie motioned her in, setting her coffee aside. "What's going on?"

Angela stepped inside and shut the door behind her. Her normally mild manner was laced with tension today, and she didn't waste time with pleasantries. She laid the folder on Cassie's desk and opened it.

"I've been going through the files the SBI cleared from Russell's office," she began. "They opened the locked drawer—remember? And turned everything over to us after determining the contents were related to town finances."

Cassie nodded. "Right. I remember that. What did they miss?"

Angela flipped through a few pages and pulled out a typed spreadsheet, neatly organized with codes, vendors, and dollar amounts. She pointed to the columns as she spoke.

"These line items don't match anything in the municipal budget. They're coded in a way that doesn't fit our standard format. And they're not tied to known vendors we contract with for town services—no licensing records, no procurement files, no standard identifiers."

Cassie's brows drew together. "So... what are they?"

60

"That's just it. I don't know." Angela leaned forward. "The amounts are *huge*, Cassie. Not just petty cash or discretionary spending. We're talking transfers in the tens of thousands. Some of them recurring—monthly. Others are lump sums that look more like seed money."

Cassie scanned the numbers. "Could it be payroll?"

Angela shook her head. "Not unless we hired a secret department that reports to no one. And there's more..."

She pulled out a small slip of paper—a printed transaction receipt tied to one of the larger sums. At the bottom was a line of text Cassie couldn't immediately place.

Mariner Holdings – Disbursement Fund

Cassie blinked. "That's not a town account."

"No," Angela said quietly. "That's a private investment firm based in Charlotte."

She let the words hang there before continuing.

"This looks like a business budget, Cassie. Maybe even startup capital. Not anything resembling household finances. These aren't groceries or mortgage payments. This is structured, layered financial planning. Someone was building something."

Cassie sat back in her chair, absorbing the weight of the revelation. "Did Russell ever mention owning a company outside of this office?"

Angela shook her head. "Never. And I was his deputy for four years. If he was running something else, he did it completely off-books."

Cassie tapped the folder lightly, her mind racing. "Could it be a side consulting firm? Something he kept quiet about?"

"Maybe," Angela admitted. "But there are no tax filings for a Russell Wallen enterprise—not in this county. I checked state records this morning, too. Nothing under his name."

"Then who's receiving the funds?"

Angela hesitated. "That's where it gets even more interesting. One of the deposit accounts used the name V.A. Financial Group."

Cassie's heart skipped. "V.A.... as in Valerie Austin?"

Angela raised an eyebrow. "That's what I thought. But it could just be a coincidence. The name could mean anything. Victory Alliance. Vanguard Associates. There's no official filing in the Secretary of State database for it—not in North Carolina."

Cassie rubbed her temple. "Could Russell have been funneling money through ghost accounts?"

"If he was," Angela said carefully, "then either someone else was in on it... or he was preparing for something."

Cassie leaned forward again. "Keep digging. Quietly. I don't want this turning into another online feeding frenzy until we know what we're dealing with."

Angela nodded, gathered the paperwork, and rose to leave.

As she reached the door, she paused. "Cassie?"

"Yes?"

"I liked Russell. I still do. But if he was doing something shady... we need to be honest about it. For the town. And for Patrice."

Cassie met her gaze and gave a solemn nod. "We will be."

When the door closed, Cassie sat for a long moment, staring out the window.

Russell Wallen had survived a corrupt administration, helped bring down a crooked mayor, and cleaned up years of financial mess.

But what if...

he'd been quietly creating a new one all along?

15

The cardboard boxes came in stacked two high, labeled with yellow evidence tags and chain-of-custody forms affixed to the lids. Quentin watched as they were wheeled into his downtown Asheville office on a handcart by a solemn young SBI clerk, who said little aside from, "Delivery for defense counsel—per authorization."

Emily signed the receipt while Abigail cleared a long conference table, moving notebooks and legal pads aside to make space. The weight of the boxes wasn't just physical. This was the full scope of what the state had compiled so far: photographs, witness lists, autopsy results, gunshot trajectory analysis, audio transcriptions of Patrice's initial intake, even Russell's phone records—redacted but substantial.

Quentin stood quietly at the table, his hand resting on the topmost lid.

"All right," he said, drawing in a long breath. "Let's see what we're up against."

Emily sliced open the first box with a letter opener, revealing thick binders of case notes, itemized inventories, and surveillance logs. Abigail started reading aloud from the top folder.

"Crime scene report from Wren Hollow Trail—states a single bullet wound, entry point chest center-left, no defensive wounds on the deceased. Says Patrice was found with the firearm, standing several feet from the body. No prints on the gun aside from hers and his."

"No surprise there," Quentin murmured, flipping through another folder. "But let's see how much they left out."

As Abigail and Emily sorted through the discovery, Quentin moved to his desk, opened a drawer, and pulled out a new folder of

63

his own. He walked it back to the table and laid it down beside the state's box.

"What's that?" Abigail asked.

"Time to let them know we're not playing defense—we're going on the offensive."

He opened the folder to reveal a signed affidavit, Patrice's medical release forms, and a formal Notice of Intent to Subpoena Medical Records from Galen Valley Regional Medical Center.

Emily's eyes widened slightly. "This is for the ER visits?"

Quentin nodded. "Both of them. Patrice gave full permission to pull everything—records, photos, notes, staff witness lists. She's done hiding."

"Do you think the state will push back?" Abigail asked.

"Of course," he replied. "But once we show that the records exist, and that there's hospital documentation of physical abuse—visible injuries, photographs, and notes from medical personnel advising her to press charges—they won't be able to ignore it."

"And if they try?" Emily asked.

Quentin gave a sharp smile. "Then we force the public narrative to pivot."

But the public narrative didn't pivot—it *erupted*.

News of the subpoena reached the Conrad estate before the ink had time to dry.

By that afternoon, Joyce Conrad had taken to Facebook with the precision of a woman used to having her voice heard. She posted a long statement, written in stark black font over a white background:

"Let me be clear. If ANYONE at Galen Valley Regional Medical Center dares to lie and say that my son Russell Wallen laid a hand on that woman, we will pursue every legal option available. Patrice Austin Wallen has always had a manipulative streak. It would not surprise me in the least if she had people inside the hospital willing to fabricate records or statements to protect her pathetic attempt at self-defense.

My son was a gentleman. A devoted husband. A faithful public servant. This smear campaign will not go unchallenged. We are already speaking with attorneys regarding potential lawsuits against the hospital, its staff, and anyone who dares to try and tarnish the good name of a man who can no longer defend himself."

Within hours, the post had been shared over 1,800 times.

Screenshots flooded Instagram and TikTok. Local influencers reposted the message with hashtags like #JusticeForRussell and #ProtectHisLegacy.

A few medical staff at Galen Valley Regional even received anonymous messages warning them not to "lie for the woman who murdered her husband." Others posted vague subtweets hinting at increased internal tension.

Quentin's office phone rang three times in the next hour—two reporters and one legal rep from the hospital's risk management team.

In the corner of the conference room, Abigail scrolled through her phone with narrowed eyes. "She's throwing threats like rice at a wedding," she muttered.

Quentin remained calm as he leafed through the release documents. "Let her scream. That's not a strategy. It's desperation."

"But she's powerful," Emily warned. "She'll turn this town upside down if it helps protect her son's image."

Quentin looked up. "And we're not trying to destroy it. We're trying to tell the *truth*. If Russell was hurting his wife, the public deserves to know. Not to shame him. But to finally understand what pushed this to the breaking point."

Abigail crossed her arms. "And what about the hospital staff? If they get cold feet from this kind of intimidation, what then?"

Quentin's eyes sharpened. "Then we remind them that truth is a defense to defamation. And I'll walk into that courtroom with or without them. But if they stand with us, we'll finally have the piece of the puzzle the public can't ignore."

Emily looked back down at the boxes of state discovery. "We're going to need a bigger table."

16

Cassie leaned back in her chair at Town Hall, the late afternoon sun casting slanted beams across her desk. Angela sat across from her, a legal pad balanced on her lap and a pen hovering just above the paper. Cassie's phone rested between them on speaker, its screen lit with the name of a town council member and the timer ticking upward.

"Thanks again, Eli," Cassie said smoothly into the phone. "Just wanted to make sure we're all on the same page before anything moves forward. Appreciate your time."

"No problem, Mayor," came the reply. "Let me know if you need anything else."

The call ended with a soft click.

Cassie glanced at Angela. "That's four down."

Angela gave a nod, flipping to a fresh page. "Anything?"

"Nothing helpful yet," Cassie murmured. "But you know how they are—get them all in the same room, and suddenly no one remembers a thing. Better to catch them one-on-one, before they start whispering among themselves."

Angela smirked. "Council politics 101."

Cassie tapped the next number into her phone and pressed speaker again.

"Donna Tran," came the cheerful voice after two rings.

"Hi, Donna—it's Cassie."

"Oh, hi! Everything okay?"

"I hope so," Cassie said diplomatically. "I'm reaching out to all the council members today to give you a heads-up. Angela and I have been reviewing some of the files the SBI cleared from Russell's office. There are some financial transactions that don't match our known records—coded differently, large amounts, recurring payments."

"That sounds… unusual," Donna said cautiously.

"It is," Cassie agreed. "One thing that came up in the files was a reference to an entity called V.A. Financial Group. Does that ring any bells?"

There was a pause. Then:

"Actually… yes. Sort of," Donna said, her voice brightening with recollection. "A few years back—maybe four, maybe five?—there was a woman who came through and met with Denise Carrow and Russell. Her name was… Veronica Altameda, I think. She gave this big presentation on how municipalities should modernize their investment strategies. Said we were sitting on idle capital that could be used to build infrastructure reserves. She made it sound very savvy."

Cassie sat forward in her chair. "Veronica Altameda. And she worked with a group?"

"I'm almost certain it was called the VA Financial Group. That's what she called it when she handed out pamphlets. I remember because I joked to someone that it sounded like a veterans' organization."

Angela scribbled quickly.

"Great information, Donna," Cassie said. "Thanks so much."

"Happy to help. Let me know if anything else comes up."

After the call ended, Cassie turned to Angela.

"Do you remember anyone by that name? Veronica Altameda?"

Angela shook her head slowly. "No. But if she came in during Denise's term, that would've been early on—before I worked directly under Russell."

"Okay. Let's divide and conquer," Cassie said, standing and walking around her desk. "You check the archives. Go back through anything from Denise's years in office—council minutes, external consultant logs, investment meetings. See if her name shows up."

Angela nodded. "On it."

"And I'll see what I can find on my side. VA Financial Group, Veronica Altameda, whatever connections might still exist."

Angela stood. "We might be onto something here, Cass. This could explain a lot."

"I think it does," Cassie murmured, her mind already racing ahead. "I just don't know yet whether it explains something unethical... or something criminal."

Angela left with her notes in hand, her heels echoing lightly down the hallway.

Once the door shut, Cassie reached for her personal cell phone and dialed the one person she trusted to dig deeper than any government website or council archive ever could.

Natalie picked up on the second ring.

"Hey, you. What's going on?"

"Think you can swing by the house tonight?" Cassie asked. "I need a favor."

Natalie didn't hesitate. "I'll be there after dinner."

Cassie hung up and stared at the phone in her palm for a moment.

Whatever V.A. Financial Group had been—whatever it was now—it had left a shadow on Galen Valley's books.

And she intended to find out just how deep it ran.

17

Abigail stood in the administrative wing of Galen Valley Regional Medical Center, her breath visible in the early morning chill that clung to the sterile hallway. In her hand were two crisp, court-authorized subpoenas: one for medical records, the other for the names of attending medical personnel present during Patrice Wallen's two ER visits in the summer of two years prior.

The records clerk—an older woman with cat-eye glasses and no time for pretense—scanned the forms, her lips pursing as she flipped pages.

"These are in order," she said finally, standing up. "Give me about ten minutes. I'll pull what we have from the archives. The records are sealed but not restricted with the subpoena."

"Thank you," Abigail replied, her tone professional but warm.

As she waited, she scanned the framed photographs along the wall—doctors receiving awards, ribbon cuttings for the new cardiac wing, the staff softball team from a few years back.

The clerk returned with a heavy file folder and a printed manifest. "You'll want this," she said, handing Abigail the manifest first. "It lists everyone logged into Patrice Wallen's files during both visits—doctors, nurses, on-duty staff."

Abigail flipped through it. Two names repeated: Dr. Clay Moreau and Lorinda Rooney.

The latter jumped out immediately.

"Lorinda Rooney?" Abigail asked.

The clerk chuckled. "Oh, yes. Everyone here remembers her. Fierce. Detail-oriented. Took better notes than half the physicians."

"She still work here?"

"No, no. She left shortly after that second visit. Got engaged to someone—one of those Beaumont men. The youngest, I think. Ridge. I believe they got married a while back, not really sure."

Abigail blinked. "As in... *Sage Manor* Beaumonts?"

"The very ones." The woman leaned closer with a smile. "Let's just say she's not clocking in around here anymore. Pretty sure she's in garden club mode now."

Abigail smiled politely, but her heart was pounding. "Do you remember if she documented anything from Patrice's visits?"

The clerk raised an eyebrow. "You'd better believe it. She took pictures, logged every injury in detail, and even put in a formal note recommending that law enforcement be contacted but the patient refused to cooperate and cited fear of retaliation."

Abigail's smile faded. "Thank you. This is exactly what I needed."

Back at Quentin's office, the team was gathered in the conference room, coffee in hand and tension in the air.

Abigail set the folder on the table and pulled out the staff manifest, tapping Lorinda's name.

"She was the attending nurse during the second visit. She's the one who took photos, logged the injuries, and filed a note recommending law enforcement intervention."

"Do we know where she is now?" Emily asked, already typing on her laptop.

"We do," Abigail said with a faint smile. "She's married to Ridge Beaumont."

Quentin's eyebrows lifted. "You're kidding."

Abigail shook her head. "I confirmed it with the hospital records clerk. She left the hospital not long after Patrice's visit. Married Ridge. Hasn't been seen in scrubs since."

Quentin stood, crossed the room, and pulled his phone from his pocket.

"What are you doing?" Emily asked.

Quentin didn't answer right away. He dialed a number from memory and pressed the phone to his ear. After two rings, someone picked up.

"Ridge. Hey, it's Quentin."

Abigail and Emily exchanged looks.

A pause.

"I know it's been a while," Quentin continued. "No, everything's good. Well… it's complicated. I've got a case—domestic violence defense. The woman, Patrice Wallen, was seen by your wife during her second ER visit. Lorinda took detailed notes. She may have been the only medical professional who tried to advocate for the patient at the time."

Another pause.

Quentin's face softened. "No, Ridge. I didn't know. That's terrible. Look, I wouldn't ask if it wasn't important. Her testimony could change everything for this woman."

He listened for a long beat.

Then, finally: "Thank you, my friend. We'll see you in thirty."

He ended the call and turned to face the team.

"They'll be here in half an hour," Quentin said. "Lorinda is more than willing to testify."

Emily nearly dropped her pen. "*Whoa.*"

"That's not just a witness," Abigail said, grinning. "That's a power move."

"You're telling me," Emily said, stunned. "And the Conrads think *they* have influence?"

Quentin sat back down, folding his hands. "The Beaumonts never get involved. Not publicly. Not politically. But when they do? People pay attention."

Abigail opened the folder and pulled out the hospital photos, gently sliding them across the table. "Well, now they've got a reason to."

Quentin looked down at the images—red swelling on Patrice's jawline, bruises around her eyes and neck, defensive wounds along her forearms.

It wasn't hearsay.

It wasn't a theory.

It was evidence.

The court of public opinion had painted Patrice as a cold-blooded killer. But the courtroom? The courtroom was about to meet the truth.

18

The elevator chimed softly as it arrived at the third floor of the downtown Asheville building that housed Quentin Stiles' law office. The doors opened, and Ridge Beaumont stepped out first, tall and grounded, his signature understated confidence wrapped in worn leather and denim. Beside him, Lorinda moved with quiet purpose—her coat belted neatly, her long curls swept back, and her eyes sharp with clarity and intent.

Quentin greeted them at the reception desk with a warm handshake.

"Ridge. Lorinda. Thank you both for coming."

"We wouldn't have stayed away," Ridge replied.

Emily peeked out from the conference room, nodding to Lorinda as she entered with Ridge at her side. Abigail was already there, tablet open, a quiet smile playing at the corners of her mouth as she slid a folder across the table toward Lorinda.

"These are copies of Patrice's ER visit notes. You'll recognize your handwriting," Abigail said.

Lorinda opened the folder slowly, scanning the page. Her fingers brushed lightly over the edge of the photo paper—grainy but clear images of Patrice's bruised face and arms, dated and timestamped.

She exhaled softly. "I remember everything."

"You were the attending nurse for her second visit," Quentin said. "You documented the injuries. You advised her to press charges. You even logged the refusal and her explanation about fearing retaliation."

"I did," Lorinda said. "I knew the moment I saw her that it wasn't a fall or a household accident. She looked like someone who'd been cornered and hit with intent. And not for the first time."

"Would you be willing to testify to that in court?" Quentin asked, meeting her eyes.

Lorinda nodded without hesitation. "Yes."

Ridge reached over and gently took her hand. "She wanted to do it back then. She just told me on the ride here how upset she was when Patrice refused to press charges. It's haunted her."

"It won't haunt me anymore," Lorinda said, her voice firm. "If I can help give Patrice a fighting chance... I'm in."

Quentin nodded, visibly relieved. "This changes everything. The jury needs to hear this from someone who saw the truth—before any of this happened."

As the team began discussing timelines and preparing documentation, Emily's phone buzzed on the table.

She picked it up, frowned, then opened her social media feed.

"Uh... Quentin?" she said cautiously. "You're going to want to see this."

She turned the phone around and showed the screen.

There, in full view, was Joyce Conrad's newest Facebook post:

"Now they're dragging that retired nurse into it—Lorinda Beaumont of all people. As if her word means more than my son's reputation. People forget who the Beaumonts really are. Money talks. And they've decided to use theirs to help a liar get away with murder."

A long pause followed.

Abigail snorted. "She really doesn't know when to quit."

Quentin, meanwhile, was already watching the comments pile up in real time beneath Joyce's post. But this time... something was different.

The top-liked comment read:

"If the Beaumonts are getting involved, I'm listening. They don't stick their necks out for just anyone."

Followed by:

"Maybe there's more to Russell than his mama wants us to believe."

"Time to let justice run its course. The lady from Sage Manor isn't the type to lie."

"Joyce, you're making this worse for your family. Back off."

Emily looked stunned. "The tide's turning."

"They've defended her long enough," Abigail said. "But going after Lorinda? That was a mistake."

Quentin turned to Lorinda. "You still comfortable stepping into this?"

She smiled faintly. "If Joyce Conrad's biggest threat is a Facebook post, I'll survive."

Ridge reached into his coat pocket and pulled out a card, sliding it across the table to Quentin. "Here's the contact for our legal team. They'll be reviewing everything Lorinda documented during her employment. They'll want to coordinate with you prior to trial."

"Thank you," Quentin said. "Truly."

As Ridge and Lorinda stood to leave, Quentin followed them to the door. Before they stepped into the hallway, he paused.

"You both know what this means. Once this goes to trial, you'll be in the middle of it."

Ridge gave a calm nod. "Then let's make sure the middle leads somewhere that matters."

And with that, the Beaumonts stepped into the storm.

Only this time, the wind was shifting.

19

Cassie popped the cork on a bottle of Pinot Noir and filled two glasses while Natalie browsed the dessert tray Cassie had laid out on the kitchen island—pecan tarts, lemon bars, and a chocolate ganache so rich it looked like it could keep a secret.

"I'll take one of each," Natalie joked, reaching for the chocolate first. "I had three granola bars and a string cheese today. This is an upgrade."

Cassie laughed as she passed her a glass of wine. "Dinner of champions."

They moved into the cozy sitting room near the fireplace, each curling into opposite corners of the oversized sectional. The fire crackled, the soft lamplight glowing against the wine in their glasses.

Cassie took a sip, exhaled, then leaned in. "Okay. I need a favor."

Natalie smirked. "You always do when you feed me."

Cassie set down her glass and folded her hands. "I need help looking into someone. A woman named Veronica Altameda and her group—V.A. Financial Group."

Natalie's smile faltered—then widened.

It grew until her eyebrows lifted and she leaned back slowly, blinking.

"Oh my God," she whispered. "Are you serious?"

Cassie's brows knit. "Why? Do *you* know her?"

Natalie grinned like the cat that had finally caught the canary. "I don't know her personally. But I've been *deep-diving* into V.A. Financial Group for the last two weeks. I've had this hunch they were connected to an offshore pipeline I'm investigating for a financial corruption story I'm building. I knew it had local ties—Charlotte, Asheville, possibly even Raleigh—but I never imagined it would lead me here. *To you.*"

Cassie blinked. "Well… that's why I called you."

Natalie laughed in disbelief. "You called me to help track something I'm *already* tracking. That's wild."

Cassie leaned forward. "Okay, you've got to tell me—how are you involved in this?"

Natalie hesitated, swirling the wine in her glass. "You know I've been under NDAs lately, but now that you've handed me half the puzzle… maybe we can talk in hypotheticals."

"Hypotheticals," Cassie echoed, smiling. "I can work with that."

Natalie nodded. "So let's say there's this investigative journalist—me—who gets a tip about a boutique investment group funneling unusually high sums of money through dormant municipal accounts in mid-size towns across the Southeast. Let's say this group markets itself as an infrastructure planning and reserve-building consultancy—smart, sexy buzzwords, right?"

Cassie's eyes widened. "That's *exactly* what Donna Tran said they pitched to Denise and Russell."

"Bingo." Natalie pointed her wine glass at her. "And let's also say that this journalist discovers that most of these accounts go quiet within twelve to eighteen months—except for one."

Cassie leaned in. "Let me guess. Galen Valley."

"Ding ding." Natalie nodded. "And now, let's say this same journalist just needed to figure out who on the inside was helping them stay under the radar, because V.A. doesn't leave fingerprints. No LinkedIn, no office addresses. Just a digital shell."

Cassie sat back, stunned. "And now you know it was Russell."

Natalie's face softened. "He's your missing link."

Cassie let out a slow breath. "He had locked files in his office—Angela just found them. Large transactions. Recurring payments. Weird vendor names. We thought it might've been a side business, but it was too big. Like corporate-sized budgeting."

Natalie grabbed her phone and began scrolling. "Do you have any of the transaction dates?"

"Angela does. I'll get them to you tomorrow."

"Perfect. If we overlay them with the accounts I've been watching, we can see if funds were being redirected. If Russell was helping them—knowingly or unknowingly—we may be looking at something much bigger than just bad budgeting."

Cassie sat in silence for a moment, then looked at Natalie.

"So... how much can you tell me now?"

Natalie looked up, her expression sober.

"Enough to say this: V.A. Financial Group is involved in at least three ongoing federal investigations—one of which I've been consulting on quietly. They present as legit on the surface—investment consulting, capital strategy—but their real operation is way more complicated. Think shell companies, offshore disbursements, and laundering clean money through clean towns like Galen Valley."

Cassie's heart sank. "You think Russell knew?"

Natalie took a sip of wine. "I think... he might've started out thinking it was just creative investing. But the question is—did he realize what it really was? And if he did... did he try to back out?"

"Which would explain the hidden files."

"Exactly."

Cassie was quiet for a long moment.

Then: "We're not just dealing with a domestic violence case anymore."

Natalie's voice dropped. "We're dealing with a conspiracy."

Cassie leaned back against the cushions, the weight of it all crashing down on her like a wave.

First a murder.

Now, a hidden money trail.

And somewhere, in the middle of it all, a woman who'd been trying to escape long before anyone even knew she was trapped.

20

The low buzz of fluorescent lights overhead was the only sound in the sterile holding room when Quentin walked in.

Patrice Wallen sat at the table, wrapped in her jail-issued sweater, eyes shadowed with fatigue but alert. She looked up as Quentin entered, her face unreadable.

"Good evening," he said gently, setting his briefcase on the table.

She gave a small nod. "Any news?"

Quentin took a seat across from her. "Actually, yes. And it's the kind that changes things."

Patrice's posture straightened. "Go on."

He pulled a folder from his briefcase and opened it, sliding a document toward her.

"This is a sworn affidavit from Lorinda Beaumont—formerly Lorinda Rooney, the attending nurse from your second ER visit two summers ago. She documented your injuries in detail, advised you to press charges, and preserved photographic evidence in your medical file."

Patrice's lips parted. "She... remembered?"

"She didn't just remember. She's willing to testify," Quentin said. "In court. Under oath."

For a moment, the silence between them thickened.

Then Patrice covered her mouth with one hand, tears springing to her eyes.

"I thought no one knew," she whispered. "I thought it just got buried."

Quentin's voice softened. "She filed everything properly, but without your cooperation, it never went further. Now she's stepping forward."

Patrice nodded, blinking fast. "She was kind to me. That night. She told me I deserved better. I wanted to believe her."

"You still do," Quentin said. "That's why we're here. And now—with her testimony—we're not just defending your actions. We're exposing a pattern. One the court can't ignore."

Patrice exhaled deeply, her voice steadier now. "Thank you. For not giving up."

"I haven't," Quentin said. "And I won't."

He stood, packed his briefcase, and gave her a faint smile. "Rest up. The fight's not over. But it just turned in our favor."

Later that evening, Cassie sat curled on her sofa in her favorite gray robe, a blanket over her legs and a second glass of red wine in her hand. Natalie, sitting cross-legged across from her in yoga pants and a cozy cardigan, had just finished describing her deep dive into V.A. Financial Group's shell companies when the back door opened.

Seth stepped inside, brushing leaves off his jacket, looking worn but wired.

"You're late," Cassie said gently.

"Yeah," Seth muttered, dropping his keys into the dish by the door. "And I've got news."

He walked into the living room and sat on the edge of the armchair, rubbing the back of his neck.

"One of my deputies forwarded me Joyce Conrad's latest Facebook post."

Natalie groaned. "What now?"

"She's going after the Beaumonts now."

Cassie nearly choked on her wine. "What?!"

Seth nodded grimly. "Said they're using their money and influence to manipulate the case. Claimed they're helping a liar defame her son to distract from 'their own secrets.'"

Natalie raised her eyebrows. "Bold. And stupid."

"The town's not buying it this time," Seth said. "Comments are flooding in—telling her to back off, saying if the Beaumonts are stepping in, maybe she needs to check her version of the truth. People are finally seeing the cracks."

Cassie sat up straighter. "Why are the Beaumonts involved? Did Lorinda—?"

"She's testifying," Seth confirmed. "Quentin has her affidavit and everything. Turns out she was the nurse on Patrice's second ER visit—the one where she showed up with facial bruises, broken ribs. Lorinda tried to get her to press charges, but Patrice refused. Still, Lorinda documented it all. Labeled it as suspected domestic abuse."

"And now that documentation is coming to light," Natalie said, eyes wide.

"Exactly," Seth said. "Quentin has it. And with Lorinda backing it up in person... that's hard to ignore. Especially for a jury."

Cassie leaned back, letting the fire's warmth settle into her bones.

"Then maybe," she said softly, "we're finally heading toward the truth."

She turned her gaze toward Seth, her voice gentle but direct. "How are you feeling... with all of this? Finding out that Russell wasn't the good husband you thought he was?"

Seth rubbed his thumb along the side of his mug, silent for a beat. "It's hard," he admitted. "He was one of the guys. We fished together. Joked around. I never saw any signs. Nothing that made me question who he was when he wasn't around us."

Cassie nodded, her heart aching with the weight of it all. "I'm finding out he wasn't the standup finance director I thought he was either. There are... things in his files, Seth. Transactions that don't make sense. Locked folders. Private accounts. He was hiding some-thing—maybe more than one something."

Seth looked up, meeting her eyes. "So we both got fooled."

"Yeah," she said quietly. "We did."

The fire crackled between them, and Natalie—who had stayed re-spectfully quiet during the exchange—finally spoke.

"Well," she said, "the truth may be slow, but it's coming. And it's louder than Joyce Conrad's Facebook feed."

Cassie let out a soft laugh, one hand resting over Seth's. "Let's just hope we're ready for all of it when it finally arrives."

21

The heavy velvet drapes in the Conrad sitting room were drawn shut, casting the room in a dusky gold glow from the antique floor lamps. Joyce Conrad sat stiffly on the edge of the tufted chaise near the fireplace, her silk blouse crisp, her phone face-down on the marble coffee table. A brandy glass sat untouched beside it, the amber liquid barely rippling.

Across from her, Lawrence Conrad sat in his high-backed leather chair, reading glasses low on his nose, the day's news still folded on his lap. He was watching her more than the headlines.

"You've been quiet for longer than usual," he said finally, removing his glasses.

Joyce let out a slow breath, the kind that sounded more like surrender than exhale. "Have I?"

"You have."

She didn't answer at first. Her eyes lingered on the fireplace, though no flames flickered tonight. She hated this kind of silence—thick and too full of truth.

"They're turning on us," she said finally. "On me."

Lawrence set his glasses aside. "You mean the town?"

She gave a bitter nod. "The town. The media. The internet. Everyone. That nurse, Lorinda—*a Beaumont,* no less—plans to testify. They've all decided that Russell was some sort of monster, and I'm the villain defending him."

Lawrence leaned forward slightly. "You've made yourself a public figure in this, Joyce. That comes with scrutiny."

She snapped her head toward him. "I'm his *mother*, Lawrence. Who else was going to protect his memory? Certainly not that woman who shot him. Not the town that's now digging through his past looking for scandal. And not you, apparently."

He didn't respond to the jab. He knew better.

Instead, he asked quietly, "What if some of it's true?"

Joyce recoiled, as though he'd slapped her. "Don't you dare."

"I'm not saying I believe everything. But the photos from the hospital. The nurse's documentation. The records Quentin Stiles is digging up—it's not just hearsay anymore."

Her hands tightened around the arms of the chaise. "So you're siding with *her* now?"

"I'm saying I'm beginning to question whether we ever really knew what was happening behind their closed doors."

Joyce stood abruptly, pacing the length of the rug. "Russell was intense. Ambitious. Maybe even proud to a fault. But he was *not* abusive."

"Joyce..."

"No!" she shouted, then caught herself, lowering her voice. "He was raised with standards. He was taught to lead. To expect excellence. Maybe he was under pressure, maybe he was overwhelmed, but he was *not* a violent man."

Lawrence rose slowly, walking to her side.

"He was our son. And we loved him. But loving someone doesn't mean they're perfect."

Her chin trembled slightly, but she refused to let it fall. "You weren't there. You didn't see how that woman changed him. She made him bitter. She withdrew. They stopped coming to family events. She turned him into someone cold."

"Or maybe," he said gently, "he became that on his own."

She jerked away. "You're letting them paint him as a monster to save *her* skin. Do you think I don't see what's happening? The town is siding with *Patrice* because they're tired of powerful families telling them what to think. But we are not just any family. We *are* the Conrads."

Lawrence regarded her quietly. "And the Beaumonts are the Beaumonts. And they're stepping forward now."

Joyce swallowed hard.

"She's going to testify. The nurse. She has documentation."

"Which means we need to stop reacting emotionally and start preparing legally," Lawrence said calmly. "If we fight every detail in public, we risk losing in court. Joyce, listen to me—if any of what Patrice says is true, we need to stop clinging to denial and start figuring out what comes next. Not for Russell. For us."

Joyce's eyes glistened with something far more dangerous than tears: realization. Slowly, she sat back down.

"I won't let them destroy his name," she whispered. "Even if he did some of what they say... I can't bear to think the boy I raised turned into someone who could do that."

Lawrence sat beside her.

"I know," he said softly. "But we have to face what's real. Not what we wish was true."

The silence returned, but this time it wasn't defensive. It was mournful.

Joyce stared down at her trembling hands.

And for the first time since this all began, she said nothing more.

22

The front windows of Valley Vogue glittered with late autumn sunlight streaming through amber glass. Inside, the boutique was warm and filled with the soft scent of cinnamon candles and polished wood floors. Cozy fall cardigans hung near the register, and the latest shipment of faux suede ankle boots lined the lower shelves in perfect formation.

At the checkout counter, Natalie leaned on one elbow, sipping a fresh latte while Kathryn adjusted a display of leather belts and long plaid scarves.

"I'm just saying," Natalie said, eyes wide with disbelief, "it's one thing to defend your kid, and it's another to go after the Beaumonts on Facebook like they're some sort of regional mafia."

Kathryn snorted. "She stepped in it this time. You do *not* come for the Beaumonts unless you've got receipts, evidence, and a bodyguard. And even then, good luck."

"She accused Lorinda of fabricating a medical report and said Ridge was using his money to buy influence. On Facebook! Publicly! I mean, how delusional do you have to be?"

"She's unraveling," Kathryn said, shaking her head. "Grief does strange things to people. But Joyce has always had a flair for drama. I remember back in the day when she pitched a fit at the county gala because someone else wore the same navy chiffon gown. Claimed she was being 'professionally sabotaged.'"

Natalie laughed. "Sabotaged by Macy's clearance rack."

The two women were still giggling when the door to the staircase creaked open, and Brontë Sutton emerged, wiping his hands on a rag and muttering to himself.

"There you are," Kathryn said, looking up. "Did you find the problem?"

"Yep," Brontë said. "Marshall never tied the line in properly. It's not leaking, but the pressure's gonna fluctuate until I replace the T-joint and run a stabilizer."

"Translation?" Natalie asked.

"I'm walking to the hardware store," Brontë deadpanned. "Be back in an hour."

Kathryn smiled. "Thank you, mountain man. You're the best."

As Brontë turned to head out, he caught just enough of their conversation to pause mid-step.

"You said something about the Beaumonts?" he asked, raising an eyebrow.

Natalie smirked. "You want the gossip?"

"I want to know what Joyce Conrad's done now," he replied, folding his arms.

Kathryn and Natalie took turns relaying the events of the last twenty-four hours: the viral Facebook post, the town's collective clapback, and the fact that Lorinda Beaumont, in particular, had suddenly become central to Patrice's defense.

Brontë listened without interruption, his expression unmoving, until they finished.

Then he let out a low whistle. "She really went after *Lorinda*? Publicly?"

"Oh, yes," Kathryn said. "Tried to say she was lying. That Ridge was using his wealth to distort justice."

"Not smart," Brontë muttered. "The Beaumonts don't flex often, but when they do, it's with purpose."

"I think people forget how rooted they are in this town," Natalie said. "Quiet doesn't mean passive."

Brontë nodded. "And Ridge is deliberate. If he's stepping into this, it means he believes in what he's doing. He doesn't care about drama. He cares about the truth."

"I think the townsfolk are starting to realize that," Kathryn added. "The comments under Joyce's post were brutal—but fair. A lot of people said maybe it's time to look at Russell for who he really was... not who she pretended he was."

Brontë scratched his beard. "Well, I'll tell you this—I feel bad for Joyce. She lost her boy. That's a pain I wouldn't wish on anyone. But I'll tell you something else... if Lorinda wrote it down, it happened. She's got integrity in her bones. Probably why Ridge married her."

"Exactly," Natalie said. "She wasn't just a nurse, she was an advocate. I saw her work. She didn't back down, not even when patients were scared to speak up."

Brontë gave a quiet grunt. "If more people had her kind of backbone, maybe Patrice wouldn't have suffered as long as she did."

The three of them sat in silence for a moment, letting that truth settle in.

Finally, Kathryn said softly, "Well... I'm proud of our town. For speaking up this time."

Brontë tipped his head. "And for knowing when to listen."

He tossed the rag onto the counter and headed toward the door.

"I'll be back with the good stuff," he said over his shoulder. "You'll have real water pressure by sundown, Natalie."

"I'll believe it when I can rinse shampoo without chanting prayers," she called after him with a grin.

The door jingled shut behind him, and Natalie turned back to Kathryn with a thoughtful expression.

"You know," she said, "maybe the real shift in Galen Valley isn't just about this case."

Kathryn raised an eyebrow. "Oh?"

"Maybe it's about people finally choosing courage over comfort."

Kathryn smiled as she adjusted a scarf on the rack. "Well... it's about damn time."

23

The detention center waiting room was quiet in the late afternoon, fluorescent lights humming softly overhead. The visiting area was divided by a thick pane of reinforced glass, with black phones hanging on either side of the partition.

Valerie Austin sat nervously on the metal stool, twisting a tissue in her lap. She looked older than she had a month ago—worn down by grief, guilt, and the crushing helplessness of watching her daughter suffer in a place she couldn't reach.

The steel door across the glass clicked open, and Patrice stepped inside, wearing the standard-issue khaki jumper, her hair pulled back in a low ponytail. She looked thinner, paler—but there was a clarity in her eyes that hadn't been there when she was first arrested.

She sat down slowly, lifted the phone, and gave her mother a small, exhausted smile.

Valerie reached for her own phone and pressed it to her ear. Her voice trembled on the first word.

"Hi, sweetheart."

"Hi, Mama."

They looked at each other for a long moment. So much unsaid, hanging heavy in the space between them.

"I… I wasn't sure if I should come," Valerie admitted.

"I'm glad you did."

Tears sprang to Valerie's eyes, and she leaned in closer to the glass. "I just need to tell you… I'm sorry. I should've pushed you to leave. I should've made you come home. I saw things. Not everything. But enough. And I didn't want to believe what it could mean."

Patrice's eyes didn't waver. "Because you didn't want to believe *he* was capable of hurting me."

Valerie nodded, her lip trembling.

"I kept thinking, 'She'll tell me when it's bad enough. She'll come to me when it crosses the line.' But you never did. And I—I convinced myself that meant it wasn't as bad as it looked. But that wasn't true, was it?"

"No," Patrice said quietly. "It was worse."

Valerie covered her mouth as a sob escaped. "I'm sorry, baby. I failed you."

Patrice's eyes softened. "Mama… you know, deep down… you were scared of him too."

Valerie looked up, stunned.

Patrice continued, her voice calm but steady. "You saw how he talked to people. How he could charm a room and then flip cold as ice behind closed doors. You were scared. Just like I was. Just like everyone else who saw the truth and didn't know what to do with it."

Valerie's shoulders shook with silent tears.

"I don't blame you," Patrice said. "Because now I know how hard it is to speak up when you're being controlled. How hard it is to name the thing that's hurting you when it looks like someone so many people respect."

She leaned forward, her voice a whisper against the receiver.

"But now? People will see it. The lie he was living… and the hell I was living."

Valerie nodded slowly, wiping her face. "You don't have to forgive me. I'll understand if you never do."

"I already have," Patrice said.

The silence that followed was fuller this time—less jagged. The kind that lives between two people who've finally said what needed saying.

"I'm proud of you," Valerie whispered. "Not just for surviving. But for telling the truth. For not letting him take that from you, too."

Patrice blinked back fresh tears. "I didn't survive to stay quiet. That's the only thing I know for sure anymore."

Valerie reached her hand up and pressed it to the glass.

Patrice mirrored it from her side, palm to palm with only cold glass between them.

It wasn't a perfect connection.

But it was real.

And for now, that was enough.

24

The savory scent of bubbling cheese and garlic filled the cozy upstairs apartment above Valley Vogue, winding its way through the vintage fixtures and flickering candles Natalie had placed on the windowsill.

She stood barefoot in the kitchen, dressed in a soft black sweater dress and fleece-lined leggings, her curls still damp from the long, glorious post-shower revival she'd treated herself to. The hot water—finally restored to full pressure thanks to Brontë Sutton's plumbing magic—had felt like heaven, and for once, her evening didn't feel rushed or half-lived.

The casserole dish was in the oven, the apple bourbon crumble cooling on the counter, and Baxter's favorite Red Rock Amber Ale was chilling in the fridge.

She checked the time.

Right on cue, a firm knock echoed at the back staircase door.

Natalie smiled to herself and padded across the room to unlock it. When she opened it, Baxter stood there in jeans and a flannel buttondown, holding a bouquet of sunflowers wrapped in brown paper.

"For you," he said, a little sheepish.

She blinked in surprise, then laughed softly. "You brought flowers?"

"You're feeding me," he said. "Seemed only fair."

She stepped aside to let him in, closing the door behind him as he shrugged off his jacket.

"I wasn't sure if you were serious when you said I needed a 'proper dinner'," he added, looking around. "But it smells like you weren't kidding."

"I wasn't," she said, taking the flowers and dropping them gently into a glass vase. "You've been running yourself into the ground lately. Eating gas station sandwiches and drinking terrible coffee. I figured someone needed to intervene."

He smiled, his eyes warm and a little amused. "I can't argue with that."

Natalie moved around the kitchen with practiced ease, pulling the casserole from the oven and plating two generous servings. Baxter took a seat at the small round table tucked into the nook beneath the dormer window, watching her with quiet admiration.

"Let me guess," he said as she handed him a plate. "This is some sort of hidden culinary masterpiece disguised as comfort food?"

"Close," she said, sitting across from him. "Spinach and sausage baked ziti. Heavy on the garlic, because I don't have to be anywhere tomorrow."

He took a bite and closed his eyes in approval. "Okay, I officially owe you one."

She grinned, popping open two beers and sliding one across to him. "Don't worry. I'll collect."

Dinner passed easily—conversation flowing between laughter, updates on the Wallen case, and stories from their overlapping circles in Galen Valley. Baxter talked about how things were unfolding with the SBI and the feds, how the town was starting to simmer down, how he couldn't believe what he'd learned about Russell.

"I think what's hardest," he said, swirling the last sip of beer in his glass, "is that I thought I knew him. Not like best friends or anything, but... enough. You fish with a guy, swap stories, share a few jokes... it makes you think you've got a picture of who they are."

Natalie nodded. "We all had blind spots. You especially. You're one of the good ones, Baxter. You want to believe the best about people."

He looked at her, then down at the table. "Maybe I wanted to believe he was just intense. High-strung. Smart and tightly wound. But hearing what Patrice went through? And then seeing what Lorinda documented..."

He shook his head. "It's not just disappointment. It's... disorientation."

Natalie reached across the table, letting her fingers rest lightly on his.

"You're not the only one," she said. "I had to report on stories like this in big cities. You learn the signs, the patterns. But it's still hard when it hits this close. When the villain was standing next to you all along, smiling and shaking hands."

He nodded slowly. "Yeah."

They fell into a thoughtful silence, one that wasn't heavy—just honest.

Later, they moved to the couch. The lights dimmed, the dessert dishes cleaned and stacked in the sink, the warmth of the apartment settling in like a second blanket.

Natalie curled her legs beneath her and pulled a plush throw over her lap, while Baxter stretched out beside her, one arm draped along the back of the couch.

For a while, they sat in quiet contentment, sipping the last of the beer, letting the sounds of the town beyond the window fade into nothing.

Then Baxter glanced over, his voice low. "Can I ask you something?"

She turned to him, already smiling. "Of course."

"Do you think... this thing between us—it's always been like this? Quiet and steady?"

She tilted her head. "I think it started as something quiet. Respect. Comfort. But it's grown. We went from knowing *of* each other… to depending on each other."

His gaze lingered on hers. "I haven't really let myself think too much about what this could be. Not with everything going on. But lately, it's all I think about."

She exhaled, her hand sliding to rest over his heart. "You want to know something?"

He nodded.

"I've never felt safer with anyone than I do with you. Not because you carry a badge or a gun. But because you actually *see* me. And that… scares me. But in a good way."

His hand moved to cradle her cheek, his thumb brushing along her jaw.

"I've wanted to kiss you for a long time," he said, barely above a whisper.

Natalie's lips parted. "Then why haven't you?"

His smile turned soft. "I was waiting for the right moment."

"Well," she murmured, shifting closer, "I'd say this one's just about perfect."

And then he leaned in—slowly, deliberately—and kissed her.

It wasn't rushed or uncertain. It was full, warm, lingering. The kind of kiss that said, *I've been thinking about this for a long time.* The kind that pulled two people into the same rhythm without speaking a word.

When they finally pulled back, Natalie's eyes shimmered.

"I'm glad you came over."

Baxter chuckled. "Best meal I've had in months."

She laughed, resting her head on his shoulder as he wrapped an arm around her.

And for the first time in what felt like forever, neither of them had to be the strong one.

They could just be… together.

25

The fluorescent lights inside Galen Valley Town Hall buzzed faintly overhead, casting a soft hum into the otherwise quiet afternoon. It was just past two o'clock when Natalie pushed open the front doors, a leather satchel slung over one shoulder, a coffee thermos in her hand, and purpose burning behind her eyes.

Darlene, seated behind the front desk, looked up from a file. "Hey, Nat. Cassie's in her office. Said to send you back if you came by."

Natalie nodded, offering a quick smile. "Thanks."

She made her way down the familiar hallway, her boots clicking softly against the tiled floor. It was quieter than usual—no council members lingering, no department heads shuffling through files. Just the quiet before a storm she could feel brewing in her gut.

She knocked once and opened the door.

Cassie looked up from her desk, a red pen paused mid-mark on a printed draft of a statement.

"Please tell me you've got something," Cassie said, standing as Natalie closed the door behind her.

"I've got more than something," Natalie said, setting her bag on the chair and opening her laptop. "I've got the beginning of the end of Russell's clean reputation."

Cassie's brows lifted. "Okay, talk to me."

Natalie sat down across from her, turning the screen to face the mayor. "So, I started with Veronica Altameda, trying to trace her through legitimate business registries. She's not on any public board listings, not in the state's financial consultant registry, and her name doesn't appear on a single legal document tied to V.A. Financial Group."

"Which means... what?" Cassie asked.

"Which means she doesn't exist publicly. Not as an executive. Not even as a registered consultant. But," Natalie added with a spark in her eye, "I got creative. I dug through old tax disclosures from three years ago, around the time Russell started managing Denise Carrow's financial fallout. That's when *payments* started showing up."

She flipped to the next tab. "Here—multiple disbursements from Galen Valley's discretionary reserves to a holding account called Harper & Easton Holdings."

Cassie leaned in. "That's not on our list of vendors."

"No, it's not," Natalie said. "Because Harper & Easton is a *shell company*. Registered in Delaware. Completely legal, completely opaque."

"And it connects to Veronica?" Cassie asked.

Natalie clicked again, revealing a scanned document.

"This is a leasing contract I found tied to Harper & Easton for an office suite in Charlotte. Guess whose name is on the lease as an executive contact?"

Cassie's heart skipped.

"Russell Wallen."

Natalie nodded. "And listed as a 'private municipal advisor'."

Cassie sat back, stunned. "So he was funneling town funds into a shell company... that he represented. And using Veronica as the front?"

Natalie tapped the table. "That's the theory. I also found a now-defunct website—just a one-pager with big buzzwords: infrastructure innovation, reserve diversification, sustainable local reinvestment. It was registered to a Veronica Altameda—but the domain owner listed her IP as a Charlotte business park where Harper & Easton leased space."

"So she's the face," Cassie murmured, "but Russell was the operator."

"Exactly. And that 'private reserve reinvestment'?" Natalie pulled up one more spreadsheet. "It coincided with major town infrastructure delays. Water main upgrades. Road repaving. Budget lines that should've moved but somehow... stalled. Because the funds were *diverted.*"

Cassie's stomach turned. "We were supposed to be saving that money to rebuild the town. Russell made it look like he was doing just that."

"He was using the real crisis to hide a private one," Natalie said. "And with no oversight on those discretionary transfers, he had a clean runway."

Cassie folded her arms, the weight of it all settling like concrete on her chest. "This explains everything. The locked files. The coded spreadsheets. The consulting documents that Angela flagged as personal."

Natalie nodded. "This was a long con. He built it on top of Denise Carrow's chaos and cloaked it in credibility."

"And no one questioned him," Cassie added bitterly. "Not the council. Not the auditors. Not even me."

"You're not alone," Natalie said. "He knew what he was doing. Picked the right time. Hid in plain sight."

Cassie rose and walked to the window, looking out over the square. People milled about—quietly, unaware that their trusted finance director had been leading a double life that might've buried their town in liability.

"We need to bring this to Quentin," she said finally. "He needs this before trial. It may not directly help Patrice's abuse case, but it paints a very different picture of the man she was married to."

Natalie closed her laptop and nodded. "I'll send him everything. And I'll keep digging. If I can connect Harper & Easton to any offshore movement, we may be able to trace even more money."

Cassie turned to her with a grateful smile.

"You're incredible, you know that?"

Natalie gave a wry grin. "You're just saying that because I brought down a ghost company with three cups of coffee and a spreadsheet."

"No," Cassie said. "I'm saying that because you've never once backed down from the truth."

They stood for a moment in the stillness of the office, the weight of the discovery balancing with the purpose it had uncovered.

"We're going to take this all the way, right?" Natalie asked. "No matter who else gets caught in the fallout?"

Cassie's jaw tightened.

"All the way."

26

Quentin Stiles carefully reviewed the packet of documents Natalie had just emailed him. He'd printed three full copies—each section clipped and color-coded. His fingers moved over the cover page, already worn from use, marked in bold:

Financial Summary – Harper & Easton Holdings, Galen Valley Funds Analysis

Next to it, he had highlighted spreadsheets showing discreet line transfers from Galen Valley's discretionary municipal accounts—transfers that coincided almost perfectly with delays in infrastructure projects across the town. The evidence spoke for itself. But paired with Natalie's breakdown of shell companies, leasing contracts, and Russell Wallen's name listed as a contact?

It was devastating.

"Are you planning to introduce this before the bail hearing appeal or hold it for trial?" Emily asked from across the conference table, her legal pad full of notes.

Quentin didn't look up. "I want it in the record. Now. Not just for Patrice's defense. This isn't just about abuse—it's about *credibility.* We're going to establish that Russell Wallen wasn't who everyone thought he was."

Abigail leaned forward. "Do you think the judge will even allow it?"

"If I frame it correctly, yes," Quentin said. "The financial misconduct doesn't directly explain the shooting—but it reveals motive. Desperation. Deception. And that he was already leading a double life. It reinforces Patrice's claim that she lived in fear—because he had more to lose than just his reputation."

"And more secrets to protect," Emily added quietly.

Quentin nodded, standing and smoothing his hands over the front of his suit jacket. "This will shift the narrative. If we can get Lorinda on the stand the same week we introduce this? The prosecution is going to feel the floor shift."

Across town at Galen Valley Town Hall, Angela Wilkes sat at her desk surrounded by organized chaos. Stacks of files, Post-it notes, and open browser tabs surrounded her like a paper fortress. After her latest dive into Russell's legacy files—especially the digital logs recovered by the SBI—she'd been working methodically through each folder on the hard drive they'd unlocked.

Most had been routine: budget revisions, memos, procurement reports.

But one folder caught her eye this morning. It wasn't in the primary finance directory. It was buried in a subfolder inside a personal archive labeled:

"Meeting Notes - Confidential"

At first glance, it looked harmless. Meeting dates. Jotted names. Cryptic titles.

But then she found a document labeled:

"RA+SG – Revised Strategy FY23"

She clicked it open.

The spreadsheet was unlike anything she'd seen from Russell before. Not formal. Not polished. It looked like something done late at night—stream-of-consciousness notes in one column, potential figures in another, followed by a section called:

"Risk Factor: Outside Exposure – Delay Project Schedules (SG to execute comms)"

Angela frowned.

SG?

Her mind whirled.

She opened a new tab and cross-referenced every staffer and council member with those initials. Nothing obvious popped up.

She scrolled further down the file. Another line caught her attention:

"RA instructed to maintain distance publicly. No direct transfers under RA's name. Continue layering through HE Holdings."

RA.

Russell Wallen was clearly **RA**. But this wasn't just a solo scheme.

There was someone else. **SG.**

She looked back at the note: *"SG to execute comms"*. Communications?

Angela's heart thudded as she pulled up the town's public affairs directory. Her eyes scanned the list and stopped on a name she hadn't thought twice about until now:

Sandra Greer – Communications Director.

Recently retired.

Smart. Charming. Well-liked.

And once known for managing press responses during the Denise Carrow scandal.

Angela's stomach dropped. If Sandra was **SG**—and Russell referred to her executing "comms"—this might not just be a buried name. This could be a buried partner.

She opened the file directory again and saw something else—an old, zipped file labeled **"SunridgeProposals.zip"**. That was the name of the *original* infrastructure renewal project from three years ago, the one Russell had spearheaded that mysteriously stalled halfway through.

Angela clicked on the zip file, and after a few moments, it opened into a batch of draft contracts, all unsigned—but each marked with speculative vendor notes.

One of the vendors?

Sunridge Media Consulting. Registered owner: **S. Greer**.

Angela stood abruptly, grabbing her notebook and flipping to a fresh page. She scrawled out the names:

- RA = Russell Wallen

- SG = Sandra Greer

- HE Holdings = Harper & Easton

- Sunridge Media = shell company

She didn't stop to close the tabs. Instead, she printed the file summary, shoved everything into a folder, and rushed out of her office.

Cassie was in the conference room when Angela arrived, halfway through a late-afternoon call with a state transportation planner. She waved her in, finishing the call in a few minutes, then stood.

"What's up? You look like you just ran here from the courthouse."

Angela didn't waste time.

"I found something. Russell wasn't working alone."

Cassie's breath hitched. "What?"

Angela dropped the folder onto the table and flipped it open to the spreadsheet.

"I was going through the digital archives the SBI decrypted. There's a file with notes that reference a second person—initials SG—helping him manage the risk of exposure. Handling communication strategy. Executing delays in the infrastructure timeline. And a note about keeping public distance."

Cassie scanned the pages, her eyes narrowing. "SG. Sandra Greer?"

Angela nodded. "She ran comms when Carrow was in office, then slid under the radar after she retired. But I found a set of old infrastructure proposals—unsubmitted drafts—and one of the listed vendors is a media firm called Sunridge. I looked it up. Sandra owns it."

Cassie dropped into a chair, stunned. "You think she helped him… cover it up?"

Angela sat beside her. "I think she might've been a silent partner in building the public narrative while he moved the money."

Cassie shook her head slowly. "I trusted her. We all did."

"She was too clean," Angela said softly. "No questions. No pushback. When the media pressure hit after Carrow's indictment, she handled every press release like she already knew the ending."

Cassie closed the folder, her mind racing.

"We need to tell Quentin," she said.

Angela nodded. "And you need to prepare for the fallout. If this breaks, it's not just about Russell anymore. It's going to call into question every press release, every budget revision, every timeline from the past five years."

Cassie stared at the folder, her voice steady but tight. "Let it fall."

Angela met her gaze. "You sure?"

Cassie nodded.

"We're not protecting ghosts anymore."

27

The visitor's room at the Asheville detention center was unusually bright for a late afternoon. Golden sunlight poured through the narrow upper windows, casting streaks of warmth across the dull gray floor.

Patrice Wallen sat at the long steel table, her hands folded neatly in front of her. She wore the same khaki uniform she had every day for the past several weeks, but her posture had changed. She no longer curled inward. No longer held herself like someone waiting to disappear.

The door opened with a soft buzz, and in walked Quentin, flanked by Emily and Abigail, all three of them dressed sharply, as if the courtroom was just down the hall instead of two weeks away.

Quentin gave Patrice a nod as he approached. "How are you holding up?"

She offered a small, tired smile. "Better now that I'm not hearing the word 'murderer' every time someone talks about me."

Abigail smiled softly. "That tide is turning, Patrice. And we're here to make sure it keeps turning."

Emily laid a thick file folder on the table and slid into the seat beside her. "We've got updates. Big ones."

Patrice leaned in, heart pounding.

Quentin sat across from her, his tone calm but charged with purpose. "First, the court has set the official date for your trial. We start two weeks from Monday."

Patrice blinked. "Two weeks."

"We'll be ready," he said firmly. "That's the other update."

Abigail leaned forward. "Patrice, I need you to hear this clearly: Russell's image is falling apart. His financial records have been fully reviewed by the forensic consultant we brought in, and they confirm Natalie's findings—he was funneling town funds into private shell companies. He had his own web of side operations."

Emily opened the folder and turned it toward Patrice. "This is a full timeline. The transactions line up with the moments he accused you of overspending, of failing to manage the household budget. He wasn't just controlling you emotionally—he was projecting guilt. Classic psychological manipulation."

Abigail nodded. "And it gets better. Lorinda Beaumont—the nurse from Galen Valley Regional—has agreed to testify. She treated you two summers ago and documented every bruise. She even recommended that law enforcement be called. But you refused."

Patrice swallowed hard. "I remember. I was afraid it would make everything worse."

Quentin leaned forward. "Her notes are damning. Her testimony is credible. She's respected and well-connected. And she has no motive to lie. Combined with the photos, the release forms you signed, and her affidavit—we have hard evidence of the abuse."

Emily chimed in, her voice steady. "Add to that: the financial fraud, your lack of a prior record, the psychological evaluation from Dr. Molina, and the character witnesses we've gathered from your courthouse colleagues? The narrative is shifting, Patrice. In your favor."

Patrice's breath caught. "So… you believe we can win this?"

"We believe we can prove the truth," Quentin said. "And the truth will win."

Abigail placed her hand over Patrice's. "We're going to work day and night for the next two weeks. Witness prep. Exhibit organization. Strategy sessions. We're not stopping until we walk out of that courtroom with you."

Patrice blinked back sudden tears, nodding.

"I didn't think I'd get this far," she whispered. "There were nights I thought maybe I'd just disappear in here and that would be that."

"You've already made it farther than most," Quentin said. "Now let's finish it."

They reviewed a few logistics—interview schedules, court appearance prep, and an outline of the prosecution's likely strategy. Patrice listened closely, taking notes on the legal pad they'd provided. Her face was calm, her eyes focused.

But when the meeting wound down and the team began to pack up, she reached out and touched Quentin's sleeve.

"Thank you," she said quietly. "All of you."

Emily gave a warm smile. "You're worth fighting for, Patrice. Don't forget that."

As they left, Patrice sat a little straighter.

Two weeks. Fourteen days.

Not to prove her innocence—

—but to reveal the truth.

And that truth, at long last, had weight behind it.

28

The backyard of Cassie and Seth Dixon's home came alive as the last of the late September sun slipped behind the hills. A fire crackled in the stone pit at the edge of the lawn, casting flickers of gold and orange across the long wooden table set up near the porch. The air smelled of cedar, grilled meat, and freshly baked cornbread, and the relaxed hum of friendly voices wove through the warm dusk.

Cassie carried out a tray of deviled eggs while Seth stood by the smoker, a towel over one shoulder and a pair of tongs in hand, working expertly through a batch of hickory-glazed ribs. On the deck, Natalie, Kathryn, and Margaret gathered around a makeshift cocktail bar Cassie had set up, sipping from glasses of sweet tea and lemon-infused gin.

Just beyond the porch, Baxter and Brontë were arguing over firewood stacking techniques while Brontë rearranged logs like he was building a cabin.

"Should've just let me do it from the start," Brontë grumbled. "Ain't a man alive can outstack me."

"You build fires like you're prepping for an apocalypse," Baxter said, chuckling. "We're just trying to roast some marshmallows."

Cassie watched them with a smile before slipping back inside for the peach cobbler.

Ten minutes later, everyone was gathered around the outdoor table, plates full, the smell of smoked meat and buttered corn mingling with laughter and the occasional pop of firewood.

But it didn't take long for the obvious shift to surface.

Natalie and Baxter sat a little closer than usual. Their glances lasted a little longer. Their body language spoke before either of them did—an occasional brush of fingers, a shared smile that lingered, even a private inside joke that caused Baxter to shake his head and grin like a man who'd just won a prize he hadn't dared to hope for.

Cassie caught the exchange first. Then Kathryn. Then Seth.

Kathryn raised an eyebrow and leaned into Natalie. "So..."

Natalie smirked. "So?"

"You and the sheriff, huh?"

Natalie laughed, her cheeks turning a little pink. "Is it that obvious?"

"Sweetheart, a blind mule could see it," Kathryn said, patting her hand. "The way he looks at you? You might as well be the last warm fire in winter."

A few feet away, Seth took Baxter a fresh beer and motioned toward the stone fence, giving him the silent "let's chat" nod. Baxter followed without hesitation, knowing full well what was coming.

When they stopped at the edge of the yard, Seth folded his arms. "So. You and Natalie."

Baxter chuckled. "We're... spending time together."

"Uh-huh." Seth raised an eyebrow. "Looked like more than just time being spent over there. I saw that little grin. You don't smile like that unless someone's got your heart involved."

Baxter didn't deny it.

Seth grinned. "Good. About damn time."

He slapped Baxter on the back with the familiar, brotherly affection only shared between men who'd hunted, worked, and walked through fire together.

"I was starting to worry you'd let someone else come along and realize what a catch she is."

Meanwhile, back on the porch, Kathryn was not letting up.

"He's solid," she said, gesturing with her fork toward Baxter. "Good mountain man. Keeps his mouth shut. Listens more than he talks. Not married to his phone. That's a rare combination these days."

Natalie laughed. "You sound like you're giving me a reference."

"I *am* giving you a reference," Kathryn said, placing a hand on Brontë's knee. "Don't waste him. I got me a good one, and I know what to look for."

Brontë gave a low grunt but didn't object. That was high praise, by Brontë standards.

Margaret sipped her tea, smiling as she watched the playful interrogations unfold. "I think it's sweet," she said. "We need a little love in this town right now. It's been a rough season."

When Baxter and Seth returned, Cassie handed Baxter a second plate of food and raised an eyebrow. "So, anything you'd like to share with the class?"

Baxter glanced at Natalie, who met his eyes with a soft, quiet smile. Then he turned back to Cassie and shrugged.

"Just figuring things out. But yeah—we're not just friends anymore."

Kathryn raised her glass. "To not just friends."

Everyone toasted.

As the plates were cleared and the firelight glowed more fiercely against the darkening sky, conversation turned—inevitably—to the upcoming trial.

"They've set the date," Cassie said. "Two weeks. Quentin says he's ready."

"He's more than ready," Natalie added. "I met with him yesterday. The financial evidence is airtight. Patrice has a better defense team than most celebrities. And with Lorinda's testimony on deck, the whole narrative's changing."

"You planning to cover it?" Brontë asked, his voice low and gravelly.

Natalie nodded. "Every day. I'm attending every session and posting updates on my blog."

Kathryn smiled. "Good. People need to hear the facts—not the social media noise."

"I've already got a post drafted about the media narrative," Natalie said. "About how towns like Galen Valley bury things in politeness and pretty pictures, but the truth doesn't stay buried forever."

Seth added, "The more that comes out about Russell, the more people are realizing how easy it is to mistake a polished surface for an honest heart."

Margaret nodded solemnly. "It's about time the town faced that. He wasn't what they thought. And Patrice deserves a chance to tell her story."

A quiet settled over the group. Not heavy—but reflective.

Natalie reached for Baxter's hand and laced her fingers through his under the table.

"I just want to make sure people understand," she said softly. "That the woman everyone painted as a killer was really a survivor with no one left to protect her."

Cassie raised her glass again.

"To the truth."

The fire cracked in agreement.

They toasted again.

As the night stretched on and the chill deepened, the group moved their chairs closer to the flames. Seth brought out blankets. Cassie passed around mugs of hot cider. Brontë passed around marshmallows like it was a tactical operation.

And for a few perfect hours, justice didn't feel quite so far away.

29

The offices of the Pinecrest County District Attorney sat at the top of a limestone government building just off Main Street, its windows offering a commanding view of the courthouse square below. Inside the largest conference room, a thick legal binder sat in front of Joyce and Lawrence Conrad, beside mugs of lukewarm coffee and a ceramic tray of untouched shortbread cookies.

The room was quiet except for the shuffle of papers and the soft voice of District Attorney Tabitha Welsh, a woman in her mid-fifties with steel-gray hair swept into a no-nonsense chignon and a reputation for being meticulous, thorough, and unshakable in court. At her right sat Assistant District Attorney Paul Barnes, younger, sharper around the edges, but equally intense. The two of them had built a reputation across the region for their conviction rate—and for how rarely they were rattled.

"Thank you both for making time," Tabitha said, glancing up from the file in front of her. "I know this is difficult, but we wanted to walk you through where the case stands as we finalize our trial strategy."

Joyce sat upright in her pale blue blazer, her jaw tight and eyes focused, while Lawrence leaned back in his chair, his hands folded together over a legal pad he hadn't written a word on.

"I appreciate the update," Joyce said. "It's important we know what the jury will hear."

"And what they won't," Lawrence added.

Tabitha nodded, turning to a marked section in the file. "Let me start by being absolutely clear. From a legal standpoint, this is not a case about whether Patrice Wallen shot and killed Russell Wallen.

That is an uncontested fact. She pulled the trigger. The weapon discharged. He died on the scene."

She looked directly at Joyce. "She pled not guilty at her arraignment, which is standard. But the evidence shows she committed the act. Our job is to prove it wasn't self-defense."

Paul Barnes took over smoothly, unfolding a supplemental report. "We've got three firsthand witnesses—the Ellis siblings, Cole, Clint, and Clara. They were hiking about forty yards away from where the incident occurred. They heard the gunshot and ran toward the sound. All three are prepared to testify that when they arrived at the clearing, Patrice was standing over Russell's body. She had the gun in hand and appeared calm, almost dazed."

Joyce flinched, but said nothing.

"They didn't hear an argument," Paul continued. "Didn't hear her cry for help or yell for medical assistance. What they saw was a woman alone with a man who'd just been shot—and no visible threat in sight."

Tabitha interjected. "Now, obviously, we can't say exactly what happened in those final seconds. But what we can say—and what we believe—based on the evidence, is that this was not a sudden act of violence committed in fear."

Lawrence finally spoke. "What are you saying? That she planned it?"

"That's what we're preparing to argue," Tabitha said. "We've been reviewing Patrice's journals—which were legally obtained through search warrant and entered into discovery. In them, we found repeated references to Russell's 'control,' 'cruel words,' and feeling like she was 'trapped with a man she feared.' But more notably, we found an entry dated just days before the shooting where she wrote that she 'had a plan' and that 'the trail would be the only place she could breathe again.'"

Paul opened a scanned copy and turned it toward the Conrads.

"It's vague. Not enough for a confession. But suggestive. Especially when paired with what we know about the hike."

Joyce leaned forward, voice sharp. "What *do* you know?"

Tabitha answered calmly. "We know that the hike was her idea. That she convinced him to go despite his protests. That he had borderline hypertension and was not physically active. The trail was moderately difficult terrain—Wren Hollow has inclines, exposed roots, uneven ground."

"She knew that," Paul added. "She's the one who recommended they go. And that brings us to the gun."

Joyce's mouth tightened. "It was his."

Tabitha nodded. "Yes. Registered to Russell. But there's no video surveillance. No photos. No other hikers who saw who carried it onto the trail. It was found at the scene, yes. But at this point, it's her word against a dead man's as to how it got there."

Paul tapped the folder. "Autopsy shows a single entry wound—close-range. No other injuries on Russell. No bruises. No defensive marks. The only wound on Patrice was the one on her shoulder—consistent with a fall or possible scuffle, yes—but not definitive."

Joyce interjected, her voice brittle. "You're saying he didn't try to defend himself?"

"There's no evidence he struck her or engaged in a prolonged struggle," Tabitha said. "Which supports our theory that the altercation was brief—and potentially initiated by her."

Lawrence was quiet, absorbing everything.

Paul continued, "We reviewed her intake physical at the detention center. Aside from the shoulder strain, there were no cuts, bruises, or visible signs of trauma on Patrice. That doesn't align with someone who just fought off a man allegedly trying to kill her."

Joyce narrowed her eyes. "What about the ER visits? You said you were still investigating those."

Paul nodded. "One visit was documented as domestic violence. The hospital took pictures. The other was listed as a fall. She denied abuse in both her written statement and in follow-up interviews at the time. So while one visit helps her defense, the other muddies it. Her credibility may be questioned."

"And the nurse?" Lawrence asked. "The one who documented the second visit?"

Tabitha's jaw tightened slightly. "Lorinda Beaumont. We're expecting she'll be called as a witness for the defense. She's respected. Trusted. And connected to one of the founding families in Galen Valley."

Joyce scoffed, folding her arms. "And no one questions her motives?"

"We will," Paul assured. "We've already begun preparing cross-examination strategies. We're also investigating whether Patrice shared these alleged abuse claims with anyone other than Lorinda. So far, no one else has come forward. We are trying to locate Dr. Moreau, he moved out of the country last year but is the only other medical professional that interacted with Patrice during that ER visit."

Tabitha leaned back. "In short, we're presenting a case that Russell Wallen was lured onto a trail under false pretenses, put into a weakened position due to exertion, and shot by a woman who saw it as her only way out."

Joyce's eyes burned. "She killed my son. Whatever story she tells, whatever picture she paints of him... he's the victim."

Paul nodded, firm. "That's the story we intend to prove. The facts are on our side. The law is on our side. And we believe the jury will be, too."

There was a long pause.

Then Lawrence, who had remained mostly quiet, asked the question that had been building in his mind since they arrived.

"If your case is as strong as you say... why does it feel like we're already on the defensive?"

The room fell silent.

Tabitha and Paul exchanged a glance. It was a fair question.

Tabitha folded her hands. "Because the defense is moving fast. They're smart. They're organized. And they're doing a good job shaping the public narrative—especially with the financial revelations about Russell. That's shifting how people see him. And if they make this about who Russell *was*, rather than what Patrice *did*, we have to be ready for that."

Joyce's voice trembled. "Then make them see. Make them remember who he really was. My son wasn't perfect. But he wasn't a monster."

Paul nodded slowly. "We'll do everything we can. But once the trial starts, it's up to the jury."

And with that, the meeting wrapped.

The Conrads left with their heads held high, but their hearts heavy. Outside the courthouse, life bustled on as if nothing were amiss—sunlight glinting off windshields, the smell of fresh bread from the bakery, the chime of laughter from kids near the fountain.

But the war for truth had already begun.

30

Natalie Oliver sat at her desk in the upstairs apartment above Valley Vogue, sunlight stretching across the reclaimed wood floors and a cup of strong black coffee cooling beside her laptop. Her fingers hovered over the keyboard for a long moment before she began typing, not just as a reporter, but as someone who had lived and breathed this case for weeks—and knew her words would carry weight.

Her blog's home page had already been refreshed with a new banner:

The Trial of Patrice Wallen – Daily Live Coverage from the Buncombe County, NC Courthouse

She began to type.

"Welcome, readers—both longtime followers and those just joining me for what is undeniably the biggest courtroom trial Galen Valley has ever seen.

Starting Monday, I will be blogging live from the courtroom as the trial of Patrice Wallen begins. Patrice, the now former Clerk of Court for Pinecrest County, stands accused of the fatal shooting of her husband, Russell Wallen, the late Finance Director of Galen Valley.

Three witnesses were present on the trail that day. There is no dispute that Russell was shot with a gun registered in his name and that Patrice fired that weapon. The defense claims she acted in self-defense. The prosecution alleges this was a premeditated act.

What unfolds in the courtroom will matter far more than what spreads through gossip or conjecture. We live in an age where technology allows us to shine a light in real time on the legal process—and I intend to do exactly that.

This blog will not take sides. My aim is to present factual, up-to-the-minute coverage, insights, testimony summaries, and behind-the-scenes context where applicable. There will be no speculation here. Just truth as it unfolds, straight from the source.

Bookmark this page.

Share it with your friends and neighbors.

Whether you believe Patrice Wallen is guilty or innocent—or fall somewhere in between—you deserve transparency in this case. Let's walk through it together."*

Natalie reread her words twice before hitting publish. Then she sat back, exhaling deeply.

It had begun.

A few miles away, the law office of Quentin Stiles was alive with rustling pages, clinking coffee cups, and the sharp hum of a laser printer working overtime. In the large glass-walled conference room, Quentin, Abigail, and Emily sat surrounded by binders, exhibits, and digital transcriptions.

At the center of it all were Patrice's journals—dozens of entries spanning years, each page scanned, catalogued, and now read for the hundredth time.

"I keep going back to this one," Abigail said, tapping the edge of a page marked with a yellow flag. "*Sometimes the only way to breathe is to get far enough away that no one can hear you scream.*"

Emily glanced at it and frowned. "That's poetic. Not criminal."

"Agreed," Abigail said. "But to a prosecution team looking to prove premeditation? They'll call it coded intent. Especially since the entry is from a week before the hike."

Quentin rubbed his temples. "They're building a theory. One that says she planned this—that she convinced him to go on that trail, knowing he wasn't in shape, knowing he'd be vulnerable, and then took the gun—*his* gun—and pulled the trigger. Everything else? They'll try to bend to fit that."

"But why lean into the abuse at all?" Emily asked. "Doesn't that hurt their case? If they admit she was abused, doesn't that bolster our self-defense argument?"

Quentin looked up, his face sober. "In a perfect world? Yes. But we don't live in one."

He stood and crossed the room, speaking more slowly now, like someone laying out the pieces on a chessboard.

"Here's what we have to remember. The prosecution's goal is to get the death penalty. Joyce Conrad is demanding it. She's pulled every string she has to make sure the state pushes for it—and that only happens if they can prove premeditated first-degree murder."

"So the abuse?" Abigail said. "They'll use it not to humanize Patrice—but to say she was calculating. That she used her victimhood as justification."

Quentin nodded. "They'll say she didn't want to leave—she wanted revenge. They'll argue that she didn't walk away when she could have. Instead, they'll claim she made a plan. That she chose the trail. That she baited him out there to isolate him. They'll spin the abuse into motive."

Emily was quiet for a long moment.

"But that's... so wrong. They're using her trauma against her."

Quentin sighed. "Yes. And unfortunately, it's a tactic that plays to the common misunderstanding about domestic abuse. The world still asks: 'If it was so bad, why didn't she just leave?'"

"Because it's not that simple," Abigail said, her voice hard now. "It's never that simple."

"No, it's not," Quentin agreed. "And we need to be ready for that mindset—in the courtroom, in the press, even in the jury box."

He looked down at Patrice's journal again.

"She wrote those words while surviving hell. Not planning murder. But we're going to have to make that truth ring louder than the noise."

Abigail flipped through another flagged section and slid it across to Emily. "This one too—'He watches me even in silence. Like he's waiting for me to step out of line so he can punish me with something I can't show on my skin.'"

Emily shook her head. "They're going to say that was paranoia. That she was unstable. Or manipulative."

Quentin didn't argue.

"They'll throw everything at the wall and hope the jury picks up the version of the story they want. Because when you strip the rest away, what they have is this: a woman who admits she shot her husband. And a grieving mother who wants someone to pay."

Abigail leaned back in her chair. "We have two weeks to dismantle their version. Piece by piece."

Quentin nodded. "We will."

The room fell into silence again, broken only by the sound of pages turning and the low hum of the printer as it kicked back on.

31

The large conference room at Galen Valley Town Hall had seen its fair share of town budget debates, infrastructure plans, and emergency meetings—but nothing quite like what was happening now.

The walls were covered with whiteboards scribbled in blue and green marker, dotted with names, dates, vendor IDs, and arrows that looped in dizzying patterns. Two laptops sat open at either end of the long table. The table itself was stacked with printed spreadsheets, manila folders, and three-ring binders labeled with bright-colored sticky tabs: *WALLEN–SUSPICIOUS TRANSACTIONS, GREER–SUN-RIDGE HOLDINGS, AUDITOR MASTER FILE – IN PROGRESS.*

Cassie stood near the windows, highlighter in one hand and a dry-erase marker in the other. Her sleeves were rolled up to her elbows, her blonde curls pulled back, and her eyes sharp with determination.

Across from her, Angela was typing furiously, her brow furrowed and her expression intense, occasionally stopping to tap her pen against her lips or scroll back through a long financial ledger on her screen.

"You're defense," Angela said, not looking up. "I'll be prosecution."

Cassie turned, amused. "Is this what we've become? A one-room courtroom?"

"Think of it as trial prep for the state auditor's office," Angela replied. "They'll want everything. All the files. All the flagged transactions. And both sides of the story."

Cassie nodded and paced a few steps.

"Fine. Then allow me to begin."

She cleared her throat and took on a formal tone, one that was more D.C. than Galen Valley. "Ladies and gentlemen of the state audit committee, what we present here is not just a collection of financial documents—it's the story of a man who used his position of trust to reroute taxpayer dollars into shell corporations while the town believed he was saving them from collapse."

Angela grinned. "Dramatic. I like it."

Cassie smirked. "Your turn."

Angela straightened, adjusting her imaginary courtroom blazer. "The prosecution contends that Russell Wallen, while once connected to the Carrow administration, was in fact the *primary whistleblower* in that investigation. He testified against Denise Carrow. He maintained meticulous records. He was the man who helped clean up the mess. Why, then, would he risk his name and legacy by launching a financial scheme at the same time he was working to expose one?"

Cassie nodded thoughtfully. "Because no one ever looks at the person holding the flashlight."

Angela's fingers paused over her keyboard. She looked up.

"That's the angle, isn't it?" she said quietly. "He was so involved in exposing the corruption… no one questioned what he was doing behind the scenes."

Cassie walked over to the whiteboard and pointed to a name in green marker:

Veronica Altameda – V.A. Financial Group – affiliated with Harper & Easton Holdings

"And then there's Sandra Greer," Cassie said. "Our sweet-natured, professional communications director who slipped right into retirement with not a single red flag."

Angela clicked open a second tab on her screen. "Her connections go deeper than we thought. I found three separate consulting contracts she issued through Sunridge Media in the year after Denise Carrow was indicted. None of them went through the proper procurement channels. All were signed off by Russell."

Cassie blinked. "That's… significant."

"They'll claim it was fast-tracked due to public relations needs during a government scandal," Angela said. "But the timeline overlaps perfectly with the transfers to Harper & Easton."

Cassie exhaled slowly. "He created a loop. Veronica was the out-of-town face. Sandra kept the press off the scent. And he sat in the middle, making it all look legitimate."

Angela closed the laptop for a moment and leaned back. "They're going to fight this. In court. In the press. They'll say it was a tiny remnant of the Carrow-era fallout. That Russell was tying up loose ends. Not building new ones."

Cassie paced the length of the room, marker still in hand. "They'll say he cooperated with Carrow's investigation, which he did. That he testified truthfully, which he probably did. They'll remind the jury that he kept records, flagged discrepancies, and helped us recover funds."

"And they'll use that to ask: why would a man who helped expose one financial scandal… create another?" Angela said.

Cassie stopped and turned. "Because it gave him the cover to do exactly that."

Angela opened the laptop again. "I've compiled all the questionable transfers. The shell accounts. The unusual vendor contracts. The adjusted budget entries Russell signed off on."

Cassie nodded. "Send it all to Quentin. If we don't include it in the official auditor's report, at least he'll be armed with the truth."

Angela hesitated. "Do we include Sandra Greer's role yet?"

Cassie bit her lip, thinking.

"If we don't, they'll call us negligent. If we do… it's going to open up a very public war with the former communications director of Galen Valley."

Angela looked up. "Which side of history do you want to be on?"

Cassie smiled. "The honest one."

Angela nodded. "Then we put it in."

They worked another two hours, alternating between legal phrasing and internal notes, compiling every name, date, and transaction that pointed to a deeper pattern of deception—one that the prosecution would no doubt try to brush off as irrelevant.

"They're going to say this has nothing to do with Patrice," Angela said at one point, scribbling into her notebook. "They'll say this is character assassination after the fact. A distraction."

Cassie's voice was cool but firm. "It has everything to do with her. Because Russell's character is central to the case. Either he was a beloved public servant ambushed by his unstable wife... or he was a man who abused his wife behind closed doors while laundering public money behind her back."

Angela paused. "You know the prosecution will try to twist it, though. Say it was a volatile marriage. That she was abusive too."

Cassie folded her arms. "Because that's the only way they can make the abuse narrative work in their favor. If they admit he abused her, the jury may sympathize. But if they can split the blame, they'll argue that the relationship was explosive on both sides."

Angela looked frustrated. "As if that makes her story less believable."

"It's disgusting," Cassie agreed. "But we've seen it before. The 'why didn't she just leave' defense. The idea that someone staying in an abusive marriage somehow invalidates their truth."

Angela shook her head. "They'll ignore every psychological study. Every pattern of control and fear and dependency."

"Because they have a dead victim," Cassie said. "And a grieving mother with deep pockets and a louder voice."

Angela returned to the spreadsheet, her voice quieter now. "I hate that Patrice is going through this. I hate that we're still having to explain what survival looks like."

Cassie pulled out a final file labeled *Cumulative Evidence – Financial Crimes* and added it to the center of the table.

"Then let's make sure we explain it better than they can spin it."

Angela looked up at her and gave a firm nod.

Together, they returned to their laptops—typing, flagging, compiling—two women committed to documenting every detail of the lie Galen Valley had been living under.

Because the truth was messy.

But it was still the truth.

And they were going to write every word of it down.

32

The late autumn sunlight filtered through the glass windows of Quentin's law office, catching flecks of dust as they floated lazily in the air. The conference room was neatly arranged: two chairs on each side of the table, with legal pads and water bottles set out, along with a stack of carefully prepared materials awaiting review.

Lorinda Beaumont entered first, calm and poised as always, her hair pulled back and her expression focused. Beside her, Ridge Beaumont looked slightly less at ease in his clean button-down and dark jeans, his quiet strength palpable in the way he moved—measured, grounded.

"Thanks for coming in," Quentin said as he stood to greet them. "I know it's a lot, but this prep will help us streamline the testimony."

Lorinda shook his hand. "We're happy to do it. I want them to hear the truth. All of it."

They settled into their seats while Emily entered with a tablet and pulled up the outline for the day. Abigail was out meeting with another witness, but she'd be briefed later.

Quentin took a breath and folded his hands.

"Lorinda, we'll go over your original statement, review the medical record from that ER visit, and prepare you for the questions the prosecution is likely to throw at you. They'll try to frame you as biased—wealthy, powerful, too emotionally invested to be objective."

"I can handle that," Lorinda said simply. "Let them try."

Quentin smiled faintly. "They'll also say Patrice refused treatment—refused to press charges. They'll push you to admit she didn't want anyone involved."

"She was scared," Lorinda replied, voice unwavering. "There's no protocol for fear. She wasn't being difficult—she was surviving."

Ridge glanced at his wife, pride in his eyes.

The rest of the prep session passed efficiently, Lorinda answering mock questions with quiet authority and calm articulation. When they reached the end, Quentin leaned back and tapped his pen against his notepad.

"One more thing, off the record," he said. "Any idea where Dr. Clay Moreau ended up?"

Lorinda's brow creased. "You haven't been able to contact him?"

"We know he left the country shortly after your ER tenure ended," Quentin said. "But it's like he dropped off the face of the earth once his plane cleared U.S. airspace. No forwarding address. No response to licensing boards. Not even the medical center's HR team knows where he went."

Ridge frowned. "That's strange. He wasn't the type to vanish."

"He was upset about Patrice's case," Lorinda added. "We talked about it privately a few times. He hated that she left without reporting it, but he understood why. He would've backed her up, I'm sure of it."

Quentin sighed. "He could've been another rock-solid witness. Especially coming from a male physician. It would've helped combat any gender bias in how her abuse is perceived."

Lorinda nodded. "I wish I had more information. Last I heard, he mentioned something about doing trauma work overseas. Somewhere in South America or maybe Morocco? It was vague."

"Well," Quentin said, standing, "if he resurfaces, let us know. For now, we'll move forward with what we've got—and thankfully, that includes you."

They shook hands again and walked to the door. As they left, Quentin returned to the conference table and stared at the copy of Patrice's chart one more time, a growing storm of questions still swirling in the margins of the case.

Across the county line in Pinecrest, the office of District Attorney Tabitha Welsh was unusually still for a Friday afternoon. Files were stacked and color-coded on every desk. The copy machine buzzed in the background, but all attention in the executive conference room was locked on a single screen as Tabitha and ADA Paul Barnes joined a secure teleconference with Joyce and Lawrence Conrad.

The video feed stabilized, and Joyce's sharply lined face appeared in the center of the screen, sitting next to a tired-looking Lawrence who rubbed his temples as the call began.

"Thank you both for making time," Tabitha said professionally. "We have an important update."

Lawrence straightened. "This is about the auditor's report?"

"It is," Paul confirmed. "We received the full findings this morning and have spent the last few hours reviewing it line by line."

Joyce leaned forward. "Well? What does it say?"

Tabitha glanced at her screen, then looked directly into the camera. "It confirms what the defense has been alleging. Russell Wallen was involved in multiple unauthorized financial activities. The report identifies over $1.2 million in redirected municipal funds over a three-year period, routed through shell vendors—including Harper & Easton Holdings and Sunridge Media."

Joyce's face went pale. "That's impossible."

"It's not," Tabitha said gently but firmly. "The evidence is overwhelming. The state audit found improper procurement methods, falsified budget entries, and questionable vendor contracts signed solely by Russell. The findings are classified as 'substantial misconduct.'"

Lawrence was quiet for a long moment. Then: "Is it possible for us to review the report in full before the trial begins?"

"Absolutely," Tabitha said. "Our paralegal will schedule a time for you to come to the DA's office next week. We'll walk you through every section."

Joyce sat frozen, her expression unreadable.

Lawrence finally spoke, his tone measured. "This complicates the trial."

Paul nodded. "Yes, it does. The defense will absolutely use this to undermine Russell's character. To frame him as a man with secrets—both financial and personal. And unfortunately, that will resonate with jurors."

"But that doesn't make her innocent!" Joyce snapped.

"No," Tabitha agreed. "But it does make it harder to prove premeditated murder."

Lawrence took off his glasses and rubbed the bridge of his nose. "Then we need to talk options. Because if we can't convince the jury of premeditation..."

"She walks," Paul finished.

Joyce's eyes flashed. "No. Absolutely not. I won't allow that woman to walk out of that courtroom free after what she did to my son."

Tabitha met her gaze evenly. "Our job is to present the strongest case possible. But we have to consider jury perception. And Russell's financial misconduct will influence that perception—significantly."

Lawrence turned to his wife. "Joyce... we may need to look at an alternative. Lesser charges. Negotiated sentence."

Joyce shook her head violently. "No. She's going to pay. I don't care what that report says. She shot my son and left him to die in the woods. I want the death penalty."

"Joyce—"

"She killed him like an animal. Like he didn't matter. That cannot go unanswered."

Tabitha's tone remained steady. "And we agree. But we also need a conviction that sticks. And right now, proving premeditation is going to be an uphill battle."

Lawrence looked down. "Let us review the report. Then we'll discuss."

Joyce said nothing more.

The screen went dark.

33

The scent of coffee and cinnamon toast drifted through the Dixon kitchen as Cassie leaned against the island, scrolling through her calendar for the week. Her laptop pinged with a morning reminder, but she barely looked at it.

Across from her, Seth finished loading the dishwasher and grabbed a second mug from the cabinet. His uniform shirt hung open over a black T-shirt, sleeves rolled halfway up his forearms as he moved through his routine like a man who'd done it a thousand times.

Cassie broke the silence first. "Angela and I finalized the full report for the auditor. I haven't slept much since."

Seth handed her the second mug. "I'm not surprised. That was a beast of a report."

Cassie nodded. "But necessary. I don't want even a whisper that we buried anything or played favorites."

Seth took a sip of his coffee. "You didn't. You handled this with professionalism and integrity, Cass."

She exhaled. "I just hate that the truth paints Russell in such a different light. I worked beside him for almost two years. I relied on him."

"I know."

Cassie turned to face him fully. "Have you heard anything? In your circle?"

Seth shook his head. "Not a word. But that doesn't mean much. The prosecution could be holding it tight to their chest—it doesn't help their case. And Quentin, from what I gather, isn't eager to let it hit the public until it's submitted as evidence in open court."

Cassie nodded slowly. "Makes sense. The only official response I've gotten so far was a quick message from the state auditor's office thanking us for the detail. They said both legal teams have received copies."

Seth leaned on the counter beside her. "That's all you can do, Cass. You told the truth. Let the lawyers do their part now."

Cassie looked down into her coffee. "I really want to clear my calendar and just sit behind Patrice through the entire trial. Knowing what I know now..."

Seth gave her a long look.

"You can't do that," he said gently. "Not as the mayor. Not as the employer of the man she shot. That crosses a line."

Cassie frowned. "But I know she was telling the truth. I know it."

"I do too," Seth said. "But that's not the point."

He stepped closer, brushing his hand along her arm.

"You handled the financial investigation the right way. You made sure no one could accuse you or your staff of bias. Don't throw that away by walking into a courtroom and sitting behind the woman accused of killing your employee. Even if you believe her."

Cassie sighed. "It's just... frustrating."

"I know," Seth said.

He reached out and pulled her into a hug, warm and steady.

"At least," he added with a grin, "you've got a best friend who's live-blogging it."

Cassie laughed against his chest. "Fair point."

Later that morning, the familiar glass doors of Galen Valley Town Hall swung open just as Cassie arrived. The reception area buzzed quietly with the usual sounds—phones ringing, printers humming—but Darlene stood just inside the hallway with a note in hand, waiting.

"Cassie," she said, "this came in for you first thing."

Cassie slowed, balancing her shoulder bag and coffee cup, and took the slip of paper.

"He asked to speak with you in person," Darlene added. "Said it was about a delicate situation. Wouldn't elaborate."

Cassie glanced down at the name and phone number on the note.

Fergus Greer.

Her feet stopped mid-step.

"Sandra's ex-husband?" she said aloud.

Darlene nodded. "That's what he said. He was here right when the doors opened."

Cassie stared at the paper a moment longer, mind racing.

"Clear my appointments for the morning," she said at last. "Mr. Greer will be taking priority. And tell Angela to come into my office. Now."

Darlene's eyebrows lifted. "Will do."

Cassie resumed walking, her pulse quickening with every step.

Why would Fergus Greer want to talk to her?

And why now?

She didn't have the answers yet.

But she was about to find out.

Cassie was halfway through removing her coat when Darlene buzzed in over the intercom.

"He's back. I think he was waiting outside to watch you arrive, I'm sending him your way."

Cassie straightened, quickly setting her coat aside as Angela stepped into the office carrying her tablet and a puzzled look.

"Darlene said it was urgent?" Angela asked.

"You're about to see why," Cassie replied.

A knock tapped gently on the door. Cassie opened it.

Fergus Greer stepped in, tall and square-shouldered, his hair gray but neatly combed, his demeanor slightly hesitant but purposeful. He clutched his ballcap in both hands and nodded respectfully.

"Mayor Dixon," he said, giving both her and Angela a slight nod. "Thanks for seeing me. I... I should've come in sooner. I just didn't have the backbone until now."

Cassie motioned him toward the chair across from her desk, and she and Angela took their seats.

"Mr. Greer, what can we do for you?" Cassie asked gently.

He looked between the two women and cleared his throat.

"First, I want to say—I respect you, Mayor Dixon. I've watched how you've handled this town since Carrow left it a wreck. I know what you went through to win that seat and what it's taken to clean up her mess. You've done hard things. Made hard choices. For truth. Transparency. And that's something Galen Valley isn't exactly used to."

Cassie blinked, taken aback by the sincerity in his voice.

"I don't want to go down with my ex-wife," Fergus continued. "I've kept my mouth shut for years, but I've got no reason to protect Sandra anymore."

Angela straightened, tension creeping into her posture.

"What do you mean?" Cassie asked.

Fergus looked them both square in the eyes.

"I mean I became aware a few years ago that she was involved in some shady dealings—financial, I think—with a man she was also having an affair with."

Angela gasped.

Fergus nodded grimly. "Russell Wallen."

Cassie's head shot up and she leaned into her desk, her eyes laser focused on Fergus. "I'm sorry, Mr. Greer. Could you please repeat that? I want to make sure I heard you correctly."

"You did," Fergus said. "Sandra and Russell were having an affair. Ongoing. For years. That's why I divorced her. She begged me not to ruin her career. I agreed. Mostly because my pride was hurt, and I didn't want to look like a fool. But they weren't exactly as discreet as they thought."

Angela's voice was low. "Did Patrice know?"

Fergus shrugged. "I don't know. Maybe. But I did—because I followed them. To their little love nests. All of them owned by Joyce Conrad and her husband, by the way. A beach house in Savannah. A luxury penthouse in Buckhead near Atlanta. Those were their favorites. Sandra always told me she was going on a girls' weekend. Shopping. Beach lounging. Whatever women say they're doing. But her friends would call the house for her while she was gone, and her sister once showed up at the house with a bottle of wine looking to watch a movie."

He shook his head. "Didn't take long to figure out she was lying."

Cassie sat back, stunned.

Angela was still blinking. "Do you think Joyce and Lawrence knew about this?"

"Of course they did," Fergus said bitterly. "I saw them. Having lunch with Russell and Sandra. Dinners. Joyce and Sandra shopping together in Buckhead. The mama knew."

Cassie folded her hands, trying to steady herself. "Mr. Greer, can you prove this?"

"Sure can," he said. "No video, but I've got photos. My camera timestamps everything. Date and time, clear as day. And I saved them all. In my safety deposit box at the bank."

Angela exhaled. "Quentin Stiles needs to hear this. This is *huge*."

Fergus leaned forward. "I don't want to be in the spotlight. I don't want to testify. I don't want my name plastered across the tv news or newspapers. I stayed quiet about this for a reason. I just want to give you some of the pictures and let you do something with them to help that woman."

"Mr. Greer," Cassie said, "unfortunately, you may not have a choice. In order for the defense attorney to use those photos during trial, he will need your testimony about them."

He stood quickly. "Then I'm leaving. And as far as anyone knows, you haven't seen me today."

He turned toward the door, but Cassie stood too.

"Mr. Greer," she said carefully. "I know you don't want to be involved. But could you live with yourself if Patrice Wallen spends the rest of her life in prison—or is executed—when you had the power to change that outcome?"

Fergus stopped in his tracks.

He didn't look back immediately. He stared at the door for a long beat, his shoulders tense.

Then he turned, eyes narrowed, his jaw tight.

"Damn you're good," he said, half-smiling. "No. I don't want to live with that."

He nodded once.

"I'll walk out of here now. But just know—I'm headed straight to Asheville. To see Quentin Stiles in person. That Wallen woman may have shot him for sure. But I believe she did it in self-defense."

He paused.

"And the reason I believe that… is because I saw bruises on Sandra after one of her weekends with him. She never said it, but I could see it. I think he was abusive to her too."

With that final revelation, Fergus Greer opened the door and walked out.

Cassie and Angela sat in stunned silence, the sound of the door clicking closed echoing like a gunshot.

Angela finally broke it.

"I need a second to process what just happened."

Cassie nodded slowly. "He just gave us everything. Russell. Sandra. Joyce. The whole web."

Angela looked toward the window, wide-eyed.

"This trial just changed."

34

Natalie sat in the fifth row of the Buncombe County Courthouse, laptop open, fingers hovering over the keys. Her nerves hummed beneath her calm surface, but her posture was straight, focused, and unflinching. To her left and right, the courtroom benches were packed—press, legal observers, townspeople from Galen Valley and Pinecrest, and a handful of familiar faces with barely concealed curiosity or judgment in their eyes.

Just ahead of her, seated at the defense table, Patrice Wallen looked small. Her khaki jumpsuit had been replaced with a modest navy-blue suit and a soft gray blouse, but she couldn't hide the toll of recent months. Her face was pale, shoulders drawn in tight. Still, her eyes stayed forward, alert and determined, as though sheer willpower were holding her together.

Quentin sat beside her, flanked by Emily and Abigail, all of them composed and steady, like a wall built to shield the woman who had once presided over a county courthouse herself.

Natalie's eyes drifted toward the back of the courtroom where Baxter and Seth stood against the wall alongside other law enforcement officials. Both were stone-faced, their presence not just protective, but symbolic. They were here for security—but also for justice.

The judge's entrance had silenced the room moments ago. Judge Robert Nelson, a seasoned superior court judge from Raleigh, had been brought in to avoid any conflict of interest. His no-nonsense demeanor had been clear from the moment he laid out strict courtroom rules: no phones, no whispering, no disruptions. Those who violated the order would be removed and banned for the remainder of the trial.

Even Natalie, with her press credentials, had to receive special written permission to use her laptop in the courtroom—and she could only type. No sound, no photography, no real-time social media posts. Her work would be posted as soon as each session adjourned.

She'd felt Baxter's eyes on her the moment she opened her laptop. They'd exchanged a look—brief, but telling.

You okay? his eyes asked.

She gave him the smallest nod.

Ready, hers answered.

And then the District Attorney, Tabitha Welsh, stood, smoothing her blazer, her expression confident and grim as she stepped before the jury box and began the prosecution's opening statement.

Natalie began to type.

Live from the Courthouse – Day One, Morning Session
Opening Arguments Begin in the Trial of Patrice Wallen
At 9:06 AM this morning, the courtroom was brought to silence as Superior Court Judge Robert Nelson called the session to order. Prosecutor Tabitha Welsh approached the jury with a deliberate tone and calm authority, beginning the State's case against Patrice Wallen.

Opening Statement – Prosecution:
"This is a case about betrayal," Welsh began. "About a woman who used the trust placed in her—by this community, by the Conrad family, and by her own husband—to engineer an escape from a life she no longer wanted, using violence as her exit."

Welsh painted Patrice as a manipulative, bitter woman who had become resentful of the life she had built—one supported, the prosecution emphasized, by the Conrad family, who had helped her get her first job in the court system. They reminded jurors that Patrice's clerk of court role was an elected one, requiring not only legal knowledge, but public trust. "That trust," Welsh said, "was abused. The position was exploited—not for the people, but for her own calculated plan."

She spoke at length about Russell Wallen's reputation—his work during the Carrow fallout, his partnership with town leaders to stabilize Galen Valley's finances. "This was not a man who deserved to die on a hiking trail," she told the jury. "He was trying to make his marriage work. He trusted his wife. And she used that trust to lure him to a remote area, knowing it would leave no witnesses."

Welsh acknowledged that the defense would present a narrative of abuse, but told the jury that there was only one domestic violence incident on record, and that it had never resulted in criminal charges. She claimed the "years of abuse" the defense intended to present were "conveniently unsubstantiated" and "clearly designed to evoke sympathy."

She turned back toward the jury with a final, chilling line:

"Patrice Wallen didn't escape a monster—she manufactured one. And she did it with one goal in mind: to walk away free."

End of Prosecution's Opening Statement.

Natalie's fingers slowed as Tabitha Welsh stepped back from the jury, her calm mask still in place as she took her seat.

She glanced toward the defense table. Patrice was breathing slowly, shoulders still square. Quentin leaned over and whispered something, and Natalie watched as Patrice gave a small nod, then closed her eyes briefly. When she opened them again, she stared straight ahead—at the jury, not the prosecution.

Baxter caught Natalie's gaze from the wall again. His arms were folded. His expression unreadable.

Natalie looked back at her screen.

She opened a new section of her document and began drafting her commentary and reaction—something she would refine and post during the lunch break.

Observations from the Gallery – Morning Session

Welsh delivered a carefully composed statement, leaning heavily on the court of public opinion—especially Russell Wallen's polished public persona and the Conrad family's well-known influence. The underlying message to jurors was simple: this trial isn't just about a death. It's about betrayal.

The prosecution is positioning this as a fall from grace—a woman given everything who wanted out, and chose to kill her way free.

What remains to be seen is whether the defense's self-defense claim, and the growing evidence of Russell's financial misconduct, will shift that narrative.

Stay tuned. This trial is just beginning.

Natalie paused, flexing her fingers as the judge announced a brief recess. The jury filed out slowly, the courtroom buzzing with the low murmur of spectators finally allowed to stretch and whisper.

Patrice stood, her eyes meeting Natalie's just for a moment.

Natalie offered nothing but a steady look. No pity. No judgment. Just quiet understanding.

Cassie hadn't been able to sit behind her.

But Natalie would.

Every single day.

35

The courtroom settled once again as the jury reentered and took their seats. The air was taut with anticipation, the silence broken only by the faint shuffle of shoes and the creak of old wood as people adjusted on the benches.

Quentin stood slowly, buttoned his navy suit jacket, and stepped out from behind the defense table. His gaze swept the jury—not with aggression, not with pity, but with calm certainty.

Behind him, Patrice sat with her hands folded in her lap, her expression unreadable but resolute. Emily and Abigail sat on either side of her, flanking her with steady focus. And in the gallery, Natalie, five rows back, sat poised over her laptop, ready to transcribe every word.

Quentin reached the center of the courtroom and turned to face the jury.

"Good afternoon," he said gently. "What you just heard from the prosecution was a story."

He let the word hang in the air.

"A story built on fragments. Assumptions. Reputations. Appearances. It's a good story. It's polished. But it's not the full truth."

He stepped forward one pace.

"They told you about a man named Russell Wallen—a respected finance director, a community partner, a husband. They spoke of his reputation, his accolades, his connections to the Conrad family. They told you he helped bring Galen Valley out of scandal. That he supported his wife's career. That he was kind. Helpful. Respected."

Quentin paused.

"But what if I told you that man wasn't who they thought he was?"

145

The room remained absolutely still.

"My job is not to prove that Russell Wallen wasn't killed by his wife. We all agree that he was. That Patrice Wallen fired the weapon. That Russell died on that trail."

He allowed those words to settle.

"But I'm here to prove that it did not happen the way the prosecution wants you to believe."

His voice deepened.

"I'm here to show you that on the day of the shooting, Patrice Wallen was fighting for her life. That she was chased through the woods by a man who had struck her before. That he pulled a gun on her. That he tackled her. That he straddled her body on the ground, put the barrel of that gun under her chin, and screamed at her with hate in his voice."

A gasp rippled through the audience.

"And I'm here to show you that what happened next—the firing of that weapon—was not a cold, calculated execution. It was a desperate struggle. A fight over a gun. A moment where one woman had a choice: die... or survive."

He walked slowly past the jury box.

"This wasn't the first time Russell Wallen's temper turned violent. You'll hear from a licensed emergency room nurse who begged Patrice to report her injuries. Who documented the bruises. Who tried to help."

He paused.

"But Patrice didn't. She was afraid. Like so many domestic abuse victims, she thought staying quiet would keep her safe. That silence was her shield. She thought she could manage him, explain away the rage, the bruises, the fear."

He turned back toward the jury.

"But on that trail, there was no silence left. Only instinct. Only survival."

He softened then, stepping a little closer.

"You're going to hear things during this trial that will shock you. You'll hear about affairs, about money laundering, about abuse, and about how the story of Russell Wallen—the man everyone thought they knew—was a carefully constructed illusion."

He let that sink in.

"When this trial is over, and you go back into that room to deliberate, I don't want you to focus on his polished image or his community connections. I want you to focus on what happened in those final moments in the woods."

Quentin took a step forward.

"And I want you to ask yourself—what would *you* have done? If someone had pinned you to the ground, a gun under your chin, their body heavy on yours, their rage boiling over, what would *you* have done to survive?"

He paused, voice dropping into a powerful hush.

"When you find Patrice Wallen not guilty—as I believe you will—I want you to be able to go home, close your eyes, and sleep. Because you didn't send a woman to the death chamber for saving her own life."

Another pause.

"And I want your verdict to speak louder than anything else in this trial. I want it to say: we believe survivors. We protect the abused. We see through the masks that abusers wear."

His eyes swept the room, lingering for a brief moment on the gallery.

"And for the countless victims of domestic violence who are watching this trial—online, on the news, or sitting silently in this very room—I want your verdict to send a message: that the tide has turned. That this society will no longer protect the abuser."

He turned back to the jury, nodding once.

"Thank you."

He returned to the defense table and sat down beside Patrice, who was wiping away silent tears.

The courtroom sat in suspended stillness for several seconds—until Judge Nelson nodded and called for a brief recess before testimony began.

From the gallery, Natalie's fingers were already flying across her keyboard.

And the truth, long buried, had just begun to rise.

36

The smell of roasted chicken and rosemary potatoes filled the Dixon kitchen, warm and comforting despite the tension still thick in the air from the first day of the trial. The back deck doors were open, letting in a light autumn breeze as Cassie set down a fresh basket of rolls and Natalie topped off everyone's iced tea.

Seth and Baxter were already seated at the table, both still in uniform from their long day in the courtroom. Their badges had been removed, but their shoulders hadn't quite relaxed yet. The weight of the trial lingered in every glance and pause between them.

"I still hate that I'm not in that courtroom," Cassie said as she pulled out her chair. "But I have to say, Quentin was *incredible*. Powerful words. A presence that you just can't ignore."

The others nodded.

"You would've thought the entire room stopped breathing when he finished," Natalie said. "I swear, you could've heard a pin drop."

Seth leaned back with a quiet hum of agreement. "That was the moment everything shifted. You could see it in the jury's faces. They were listening to him in a different way than they listened to the DA."

"I watched Joyce most of the time Quentin was speaking," Seth added, reaching for a roll. "Her expression didn't soften once. She looked furious. Stone cold."

"She *fake cried* during Tabitha's opening," Baxter chimed in, shaking his head. "Dabbed her eyes with a tissue and everything. But when Quentin spoke, she didn't blink. Just clenched her jaw and stared daggers."

"I didn't watch Joyce," Natalie said. "I watched Patrice. The entire time. Her hands never moved from her lap. Her eyes stayed forward, but I saw her swallow hard when Quentin started talking about what happened on that trail. I think it was the first time she realized someone was really telling *her* story."

Cassie exhaled and leaned forward slightly. "That courtroom must feel like a pressure cooker."

"It is," Natalie said. "It's intense. I'm used to high-profile cases, but this is different. It's personal to the town. Everyone's got history with one another."

Seth nodded. "The energy changes depending on who's walking in. When Joyce enters? It's stiff. Controlled. But when Quentin and his team come in with Patrice? The gallery leans in a little. They want to hear. They want the other version."

Cassie smiled faintly and turned to Natalie. "I'm just so grateful you're blogging this. I don't think people realize how important it is to document this kind of story as it happens. Unfiltered."

Natalie chuckled. "Well, I can tell you it's being read. I've gained thousands of subscribers in the past forty-eight hours."

Baxter raised his brows. "Seriously?"

"I got an email from my hosting service," Natalie said, grinning. "Suggested I upgrade my plan because of the spike in traffic. I did—immediately. Last thing I want is to crash during live updates from the most important trial this county has ever seen."

Seth let out a low whistle. "People are hungry for the truth. Especially when they don't trust what they see on social media anymore."

Cassie looked around the table, her heart full despite the grim circumstances that had brought them together.

"I don't know how this trial's going to end," she said. "But I'm glad it's being told right. Not through spin. Not through gossip. But with eyes wide open."

Natalie lifted her glass of tea. "To truth."

Baxter tapped his glass to hers. "And accountability."

Seth raised his own. "And survival."

Cassie clinked her glass to all three. "And the strength to tell the story, even when it's hard."

They drank in unison, then turned their focus back to dinner.

But in their minds, the echoes of the courtroom were still ringing—and the trial was far from over.

The following morning, the Buncombe County Courthouse was buzzing long before the judge took the bench. Security remained tight, and tension lingered just beneath the surface of every step down the marble hallway.

Natalie arrived early, her press badge in hand, and took her seat in the fifth row once again. Her laptop glowed softly as she pulled up the draft of her blog from the previous night, ready to continue her real-time chronicle of the trial.

At the front of the courtroom, the prosecution team looked sharp and ready. Tabitha conferred with Paul while organizing a stack of notes, her fingers tapping thoughtfully against her water bottle.

At precisely 9:01 AM, Judge Robert Nelson entered and called the session to order. The jury filed in silently.

The prosecution called their first witness.

"The State calls Clara Ellis."

A young woman in her late twenties, Clara Ellis took the stand with a quiet confidence, her brown hair pulled back into a braid and a light tremble in her voice. She wore jeans, a blazer, and hiking boots—as though still half-attached to the trail where everything had changed.

After stating her name and swearing in, she began.

"I was hiking Wren Hollow Trail with my brothers, Cole and Clint," Clara said. "We heard a loud noise—it sounded like a gunshot. We were about twenty yards downhill. We ran toward it."

Tabitha nodded. "What did you see when you arrived?"

Clara hesitated. "I saw a woman—Patrice Wallen. She was standing over a man... who we later found out was her husband. She was holding a gun."

"And what was her demeanor?"

"She looked... stunned. She saw us and said something like 'Please help him.' She laid the gun on the ground immediately."

"Did she ask you to do anything?"

"Yes," Clara said, voice firmer. "She asked us to get help. I knew a spot back on the trail where you could get a signal, so I ran and called 911."

Tabitha nodded again. "And when you returned?"

"Patrice was on the ground in a fetal position, crying. My brothers were performing CPR."

"Did anyone else arrive shortly after?"

"Deputy Ranger Justin Foster," Clara said. "About twenty minutes later."

Tabitha offered a brief smile. "Thank you. No further questions."

Paul Barnes followed up with brief clarification on Clara's position on the trail and the time it took for help to arrive. Then Quentin stood.

He kept it short.

"Ms. Ellis, at any point, did you see Patrice Wallen attempt to flee the scene?"

"No."

"Did she act like she was glad her husband had died?"

"No."

"Did she seem... distraught?"

Clara's voice was firm. "Yes."

Quentin nodded and sat back down.

Next, Clint Ellis.

Clint, the middle sibling, had the quiet steadiness of someone used to working with his hands. His voice was calm, but his eyes flickered with the memory of what he saw that day.

"We ran toward the sound," Clint confirmed. "Patrice was standing there, gun in her hand. She laid it down immediately."

He described starting CPR with Cole while Clara ran for help.

"Did you feel threatened?" Tabitha asked.

"No, ma'am. I felt... sorry for her."

"Why?"

"She looked broken. Like something terrible had just happened."

Quentin's cross was minimal again. He only asked two questions.

"Did she show any signs of aggression?"

"No."

"And she stayed the whole time?"

"She never tried to leave," Clint said. "She just sat there, crying."

Finally, Cole Ellis.

The eldest and most protective of the trio, Cole had a strong voice and carried himself like someone who'd seen more than he wanted to. He repeated the same account: gunshot, running, Patrice standing over Russell, the gun placed down carefully.

"I stood over it," Cole added. "Didn't want anyone touching it. But I didn't pick it up. Didn't want my prints on it either."

"Were you afraid of her?"

"No. I thought she might collapse. Honestly, she looked like she already had."

"Did she resist when Ranger Foster arrived?"

"No. Just cried. Didn't say much."

Quentin's questions, once again, were brief and pointed.

"And she thanked you when you helped?"

"Yes. She was grateful. Scared, but grateful."

Natalie's hands flew over the keys:

Trial Day Two – Morning Session Summary

Witness Testimony: The Ellis Siblings

The prosecution's first three witnesses—Clara, Clint, and Cole Ellis—told nearly identical accounts of what happened on Wren Hollow Trail the morning of Russell Wallen's death.

All three heard a single gunshot and ran toward the sound. They found Patrice Wallen standing over her husband's body with a gun in hand. She immediately placed the weapon on the ground and asked them to help.

Clara ran for cell reception and called 911. When she returned, Patrice was lying in the fetal position, crying. Her brothers, Clint and Cole, attempted CPR, but Russell Wallen had no pulse.

All three witnesses described Patrice as distraught, cooperative, and never attempted to flee.

The defense's cross-examination was minimal—focused solely on clarifying Patrice's emotional state and actions. The prosecution raised a few mild objections, but the judge overruled most.

In the end, the Ellis siblings' testimony did no major damage—or good—for either side. As one courtroom spectator whispered during the recess:

"They just confirmed what everyone already knew."

Natalie saved the post and closed her laptop gently as the judge called for lunch recess.

So far, the jury had seen grief. Shock. A glimpse of trauma.

But not yet guilt.

Not yet innocence.

Just the complicated middle.

37

After the lunch recess, the energy in the courtroom had shifted slightly—less anticipation, more tension. The kind that comes from retelling trauma too many times in too short a span.

Judge Robert Nelson took his seat once more, and with a nod, District Attorney Tabitha Welsh called the next witness.

"The State calls Deputy Ranger Justin Foster to the stand."

Justin, a clean-shaven young man in a crisp ranger uniform, stepped into the witness box with the composed air of someone who had spent his entire career playing by the rules. He stated his name, role, and how long he'd served in the ranger division.

"Deputy Foster," Tabitha began, "on the morning of the incident, were you the first law enforcement officer to arrive at the Wren Hollow Trail scene?"

"Yes, ma'am," he said. "I received the emergency dispatch at approximately 10:22 a.m. I arrived on site about twenty minutes later."

"And what did you see when you arrived?"

"I came up on the clearing where the shooting occurred. Three individuals, the Ellis siblings, were standing nearby. They immediately pointed me to the victim—Russell Wallen—who was lying on the ground. His wife, Patrice Wallen, was off to the side in a fetal position."

"Was she crying?"

"No, ma'am. She wasn't crying when I arrived. Just... staring. Her eyes were wide. She was completely still."

"And did you attempt to speak to her?"

"Yes. I checked Russell first—no pulse, no sign of life. Then I approached Patrice. I asked her if she had shot her husband. She said yes."

The courtroom stirred with hushed whispers.

"What did you do then?"

"I asked her if she could stand. She nodded and stood up on her own. I told her I was placing her under arrest for the shooting of Russell Wallen. She didn't argue. She turned around and put her hands behind her back for me."

"And after you cuffed her?"

"She collapsed to her knees. Didn't say a word. I allowed her to sit on the ground and radioed for backup."

Tabitha nodded. "Thank you, Deputy. No further questions."

Quentin Stiles stood and approached the witness box. His tone was calm, respectful.

"Deputy Foster, at any point before backup arrived, did Patrice Wallen attempt to flee the scene?"

"No, sir."

"Did she resist your arrest?"

"No. She was cooperative."

"Would you describe her as aggressive or violent at any time during your interaction?"

"No. If anything, she looked… hollowed out."

"Thank you, Deputy."

Quentin returned to his seat, and Foster was excused.

Next, the State called Rosalie Spencer, lead paramedic that day.

Rosalie was in her early forties with sharp eyes and a calm voice, wearing her EMS uniform with a professionalism that made the jury sit straighter.

"Paramedic Spencer," Tabitha began, "when did you arrive on scene?"

"Approximately six minutes after the ranger's call came through requesting emergency services," she said.

"And what did you do upon arrival?"

"I went to the victim, Mr. Wallen. We performed a full vitals check. There were no signs of life—he was already gone. We covered him and called the medical examiner."

"And what was Mrs. Wallen's condition at that point?"

"She was seated nearby, in cuffs, not speaking. She was conscious but unresponsive to questions."

"No further questions."

Quentin stood briefly. "Any doubt in your mind that Mr. Wallen was deceased when you arrived?"

"None."

"Thank you."

Jay Ammons, Rosalie's EMS partner, was the final witness before the afternoon recess. His testimony matched hers almost exactly—quick arrival, clear signs of death, no signs of struggle post-incident. He added that Patrice didn't speak to them at all but did not resist care when they checked her shoulder.

Once Jay stepped down, Judge Nelson looked at the clock and called for a recess.

Natalie's update posted soon after:

Trial Day Two – Afternoon Summary

Testimonies: Deputy Justin Foster, Paramedics Rosalie Spencer and Jay Ammons

The State continued to build its foundation by calling key responders who arrived at the scene of Russell Wallen's death.

Deputy Foster recounted arriving at the scene, securing the weapon, confirming Russell was deceased, and approaching Patrice Wallen. According to his testimony, Patrice admitted to the shooting, cooperated fully with her arrest, and made no attempt to flee or explain.

Paramedics Spencer and Ammons confirmed Russell was already dead upon arrival. They described Patrice as unresponsive and emotionally shut down.

Quentin Stiles offered only brief clarifications, asking responders to confirm that Patrice did not flee, resist, or show aggression.

These testimonies—though emotionally heavy—served primarily to confirm the timeline and facts already known. No major damage done to the defense. No new revelations. But the courtroom remains on edge, awaiting the testimony that may finally tip the scale.

38

The third day of testimony began under an overcast sky, the kind that weighed on the courthouse like a wool blanket. Inside, the gallery was packed once again—more faces from Pinecrest and Galen Valley, many now familiar, all tuned in for the next emotional round.

Judge Robert Nelson called the session to order promptly at 9 a.m. and the prosecution wasted no time.

"The State calls Joyce Conrad to the stand."

The quiet buzz of the gallery stilled.

Joyce, regal in her cream-colored suit, made her way to the witness box like a woman born to command attention. She moved with grace, her silver hair swept back, a pearl brooch on her lapel, and a somber expression fixed on her face.

After being sworn in, Tabitha Welsh approached.

"Mrs. Conrad, can you tell us how you learned about your son's death?"

Joyce swallowed visibly. "A sheriff's deputy came to our home. It was just before noon. He told us Russell had been shot... and that his wife, Patrice, was in custody."

"And how did you respond?"

Her voice cracked ever so slightly. "It felt like the ground disappeared beneath my feet."

Tabitha nodded gently and led her back in time.

"Tell us about when your son met Patrice Wallen."

Joyce's expression shifted into one of nostalgic tension. "They met at a fundraiser. I believe it was for the historic courthouse restoration. Patrice was working as an assistant for a non-profit at the time. She was charming, bright, ambitious. Russell was taken with her immediately."

"Did your family support the relationship?"

"We did," Joyce said carefully. "We helped her find employment at a state agency in Raleigh early in her career. She had no family in the area. We became that support system for her."

"And throughout her career?"

"We supported her campaigns," Joyce said proudly. "My husband and I hosted fundraisers in our home. She rose quickly through the court system. Clerk of Court is not an easy office to win. We believed in her."

"Did Russell ever confide in you about his marriage?"

Joyce hesitated. "Not in so many words. But in recent years, he'd grown… withdrawn. Less joyful. I asked once if everything was alright, and he said, 'It's complicated, Mom.' But he never said he wanted to leave her."

"Did you ever witness them fight? Or hear your son yell at Patrice?"

"No," Joyce said firmly. "He was quiet. Measured. Not one to raise his voice, especially not to a woman."

Tabitha nodded and stepped back.

"Thank you, Mrs. Conrad."

Quentin Stiles rose from his chair. The courtroom held its breath.

But after a beat, he shook his head. "No questions, Your Honor."

Judge Nelson dismissed Joyce, who stood, smoothed her skirt, and walked back to her seat with her chin lifted.

Next came Lawrence Conrad, called briefly to echo Joyce's sentiments.

He was more restrained, less emotionally vivid. He answered clearly, briefly, saying that Russell was dedicated, smart, and had never shared anything that indicated his marriage was in trouble. He did not cry. He did not embellish. His tone was factual.

And once again, Quentin declined to cross-examine.

Then the prosecution shifted gears.

"The State calls Giles Weston."

A stocky man in his sixties with a kind face and calloused hands, Giles Weston approached the stand with a slight limp. He was sworn in and adjusted his thick glasses.

"Mr. Weston, can you tell the jury about your relationship with Russell Wallen?"

"Yes, ma'am. I run the Shoreside Boys' Home, a nonprofit for boys in foster care. About five years ago, Russell showed up—quiet guy, but clearly interested in doing more than just writing a check."

"And what did he do?"

"He donated generously, sure," Giles said. "But more than that, he got involved. Took the boys on fishing trips, helped organize sports tournaments, even brought in tutors and counselors. Some of those kids don't have fathers. Russell became that for a few of them."

His voice softened.

"He was the kind of man who didn't talk about what he did. He just showed up. Made a difference."

"Was he still active in your organization before his death?"

"Absolutely. He was helping us plan a fall camping trip when... when this happened."

"Would you say he was a positive role model?"

"More than that. He's missed every single day by the boys and by every one of us who work with them."

Tabitha nodded. "Thank you, Mr. Weston. No further questions."

Quentin stood slowly.

"No questions at this time, Your Honor."

Judge Nelson gaveled for a short recess.

Natalie's blog post was already forming in her mind:

Trial Day Three – Morning Session

The Prosecution Plays to Heart and History

Today's testimony from Joyce and Lawrence Conrad painted a deeply personal picture of Russell Wallen—one of loyalty, grace, and generosity. Joyce described her family's unwavering support of Patrice Wallen throughout her career and seemed to imply betrayal not just of Russell, but of the family legacy.

Their testimony was emotional but restrained.

The standout, however, was Giles Weston, director of the Shoreside Boys' Home. His story of Russell mentoring fatherless boys brought many in the courtroom to tears.

Notably, the defense declined to cross-examine all three witnesses. A calculated move? Or a sign that this round of character-building, while heartfelt, did not shake their core defense?

Either way, the prosecution is doubling down on Russell's public reputation—in an attempt to drown out any whisper of his private darkness.

So far, they've succeeded in one thing: reminding the jury of who Russell was to the world.

Whether that holds up against who he was in his marriage remains to be seen.

After the judge's recess and a quiet, tension-laden break, the court reconvened for the afternoon session. The morning had been heavy with personal grief—Joyce and Lawrence Conrad had spoken of their son with reverence, while Giles Weston had drawn the courtroom into the image of Russell Wallen as a selfless mentor.

But as Tabitha stood once more, her eyes sharper than before, it was clear the prosecution was preparing to pivot the case.

"Your Honor, the State would now like to call Amy Glaston to the stand."

There was a barely perceptible shift in the air as a woman in her early forties, dressed in a simple gray blazer and black slacks, walked toward the witness box. Amy, Patrice's Deputy Clerk of Court, had worked at her side for years.

After being sworn in, Amy settled stiffly into her seat.

"Ms. Glaston," Tabitha began, "you've worked with the defendant for how long?"

"Almost ten years," Amy said, her voice tight. "Five of those directly under her leadership."

"And in all those years, did you ever witness Patrice come to work with bruises, injuries, or visible signs of abuse?"

Amy hesitated. "No… nothing visible."

"Did she ever talk to you about being afraid of her husband?"

"No."

"And if she were in fear for her life, wouldn't you agree she would've confided in someone like you? Someone close?"

Objection. Quentin was on his feet instantly.

"Speculative, Your Honor."

"Sustained," Judge Nelson said calmly. "Rephrase."

Tabitha nodded. "Did Patrice ever give you reason to believe she was being mistreated at home?"

"No. She was private, but… professional. Always put-together."

"And yet," Tabitha continued, turning to the evidence table, "we're now hearing that she was in a years-long abusive relationship. The State would like to enter into evidence excerpts from the defendant's personal journals."

The courtroom murmured as a binder was handed to the judge and then to the jury.

"These entries," Tabitha said, "do not reflect the voice of a battered woman. They reflect dissatisfaction. Restlessness. Regret. Words of someone crafting a narrative to justify a decision already made."

Amy blinked at the page handed to her on the stand. Her face visibly changed.

She'd clearly never seen these entries before.

"I… I don't know what to say," she murmured.

"Do these entries support the image of a woman in fear? Or a woman looking for an excuse?"

Quentin rose slowly when it was his turn.

"Ms. Glaston," he said gently, "do you believe a woman can be in an abusive relationship and still smile at work?"

"Yes."

"Do you believe a victim might hide bruises, wear long sleeves, use makeup?"

"Yes."

"Do you think fear always looks like screaming or running?"

"No," Amy said. Her voice cracked.

"Do you believe it's possible you just didn't know?"

Amy wiped her eye. "Yes. It's possible."

Quentin nodded and sat.

The courtroom stilled for a moment before Judge Nelson gave a nod to the clerk.

Tabitha stood again.

"The State now calls Winnie Franklin to the stand."

Winnie, petite and soft-spoken, looked even more rattled than Amy as she made her way to the front. Her role assisting Patrice with administrative duties during traffic court had brought her into close contact with her boss every week.

After the formalities, Tabitha dove in.

"Ms. Franklin, during the years you worked with Patrice Wallen, did you ever see bruises or physical injuries that made you concerned?"

"No."

"Did she ever express fear, discuss issues at home?"

"No. She always seemed calm. In charge."

Tabitha walked to the evidence table again. "You've seen the journal entries?"

Winnie looked visibly shaken. "Only just now."

"Do these sound like the words of a woman being terrorized at home?"

Winnie shook her head slightly. "They sound like... someone sad."

Tabitha turned to the jury. "The State contends that these journal entries are part of a constructed defense, one developed in secret to fabricate a pattern of abuse that never existed."

Quentin's cross was short but deeply impactful.

"Ms. Franklin, you said Patrice always seemed calm and in control."

"Yes."

"Is it possible that was her survival strategy?"

Winnie hesitated, her eyes glistening.

"Yes."

"Would you agree that trauma doesn't always make itself obvious to coworkers?"

"Yes."

"And if someone trusted you with their truth, would you believe them?"

Winnie nodded slowly. "Yes."

Tabitha objected to the line of questioning multiple times, but Judge Nelson overruled her—his gaze steady, allowing the defense to plant seeds of reasonable doubt.

When Winnie stepped down, Judge Nelson recessed the court for the day.

Natalie was already typing her afternoon blog post as she watched Amy and Winnie walk quickly down the hallway.

Their eyes were red. Their faces blotchy.

They didn't look like people who had just testified against someone.

They looked like people who had just seen a version of the truth they weren't ready for.

Trial Day Three – Afternoon Session Summary
State Turns to Journals, Co-Workers in Bid to Undermine Abuse Claims

In a bold move, the prosecution called two of Patrice Wallen's closest colleagues—Deputy Clerk of Court Amy Glaston and admin assistant Winnie Franklin—to question the credibility of Patrice's domestic violence claims.

Both women testified they had never seen visible signs of abuse, nor had Patrice confided in them. The prosecution then introduced excerpts from Patrice's personal journals—entries that painted a picture of emotional dissatisfaction rather than physical fear.

The aim was clear: to cast doubt on the existence of abuse.

But the courtroom reacted viscerally to the co-workers' discomfort. It was obvious neither had seen these entries before, and Quentin Stiles capitalized on their honest uncertainty. His cross-examination prompted both women to admit that not all abuse is visible and that it is entirely possible Patrice had hidden what was happening at home.

While the prosecution hoped to shift momentum in their favor, the impact of the witnesses' obvious unease may have softened the blow.

As I was leaving, I saw both women rushing out of the courthouse, tear-streaked and shaken.

The truth—whatever it is—clearly isn't easy for anyone to carry.

39

The warm glow of Valley Vogue's lights spilled through the boutique's large display windows as the last rays of sun dipped behind the Galen Valley ridge. The store was closed for the evening, the racks neat and tidy, soft music playing faintly through the speakers.

In the cozy sitting area Kathryn had created near the back fitting rooms—complete with velvet chairs, a small table, and a wine cart—the women of Galen Valley gathered to decompress.

Cassie swirled a glass of red wine while seated in a plush green armchair. Across from her, Natalie, perched on a velvet bench, had her laptop closed but within reach, as always. Margaret arrived last, placing her wrap across the back of a chair and pouring herself a glass from the bottle Kathryn had uncorked.

"I still can't get over how the prosecution ambushed Amy and Winnie today," Kathryn said, shaking her head as she settled into a floral settee. "Blindsiding your own witnesses with journal entries they've never seen? Terrible strategy."

Cassie nodded in agreement. "It backfired. You could see it on their faces. Those women were shaken—and not because they doubted Patrice. They were shocked they hadn't been told what they were walking into."

"I think the prosecution pushed too hard on the narrative that Patrice fabricated a domestic violence story," Natalie said. "It was heavy-handed. Too calculated. Quentin didn't even have to do much—he just let them walk into their own trap."

"They overshot their case," Kathryn said, lifting her glass. "And Quentin played it perfectly. Just the right questions. No theatrics."

"I agree," Cassie said. "It was honest. Grounded. Human."

But Margaret—who had been quietly sipping and listening—set her glass down and leaned forward.

"I'm going to offer a slightly different perspective," she said.

The others turned to her.

"I think the prosecution *intended* to rattle them," Margaret continued. "And in that sense, they succeeded. Amy and Winnie weren't just surprised—they were doubting. Not Patrice's pain, necessarily. But whether they missed something important. And if they missed it, what else could be wrong in the story they thought they knew?"

Silence settled in the circle.

"That kind of internal conflict," Margaret added, "lingers with a jury. They'll see it too."

Cassie frowned. "So you think it worked?"

"I think it planted just enough uncertainty to muddy the waters," Margaret replied. "But Quentin did a brilliant job reclaiming the space."

Natalie sighed and leaned her head back.

"My comment section is a war zone."

Cassie looked over at her. "Really?"

"Oh yeah," Natalie said. "It's blowing up. Thousands of comments—split almost *exactly* down the middle. One half says she's a murderer with a victim complex. The other says she's a survivor who finally snapped. And then there's the third group—people who just want to watch it all burn."

"That's awful," Kathryn said.

"I tried replying at first," Natalie admitted. "Tried to engage. Clarify. But they come in fast and furious now. I finally gave up and put a disclaimer on the blog saying I won't be responding until the trial is over."

"Smart," said Cassie.

"I also had to turn on moderation filters," Natalie added. "Some of the comments… are horrific. The language. The personal attacks. The cruelty. It's unbelievable."

Margaret looked genuinely stunned. "I never knew blogging could be so difficult."

"Normally it's not," Natalie said. "But we're living through a *tumultuous moment*. This trial has taken over the narrative. And everyone—everyone—has something to say."

"Well," Kathryn said, lifting her glass again, "I'm glad we have each other. Lord knows the town feels like it's on a fault line."

"Here's to truth," Cassie said.

"To accountability," Margaret added.

"To survival," Natalie whispered.

They clinked glasses gently.

Outside, the valley winds stirred the trees, carrying with them the heavy weight of everything still left to be said.

The following morning, the courtroom buzzed with anticipation. Most assumed the prosecution would rest their case after the previous day's intense testimony. Even Natalie, laptop open and ready, expected a short session.

But something shifted the moment Tabitha Welsh leaned over and whispered to Paul Barnes, who stood and said, "Your Honor, the State has one more witness."

Whispers fluttered through the gallery.

Judge Nelson nodded once. "Approach the bench."

Barnes, Welsh, and Quentin Stiles stepped forward, and Paul handed sealed manila envelopes to both the judge and the defense team. The private conference at the bench lasted five minutes—tense, quiet, broken only by the shuffling of papers.

Quentin returned to his table, whispered something to Patrice, and her head dropped slowly, her fingers gripping the table. He passed the envelope to Emily and Abigail, who opened it and read quickly.

Emily shook her head in visible frustration. Abigail said nothing—she merely slid the papers back into the envelope and placed it directly in front of Quentin.

From her seat, Natalie watched the exchange closely. Quentin's posture was tighter than usual. His pen scratched furiously across his legal pad. He leaned into Patrice again and whispered more, and she blinked slowly, lips pressed together.

Natalie turned toward the prosecution table and saw them now speaking with Joyce and Lawrence Conrad. The two looked nearly smug—Joyce with a slight smile, Lawrence leaning in with his usual stoic expression tinged by satisfaction.

Oh crap, Natalie thought, fingers already poised to summarize. This is not good.

She looked over to Baxter, standing against the wall. He met her eyes and gave a shrug and a shake of his head—he had no clue what was happening either.

Judge Nelson gaveled the room to attention.

"State, call your witness."

Paul Barnes rose. "The State calls Irene Hopkins to the stand."

From the gallery entrance, Irene Hopkins walked with poise, her chic updo perfect, her black pantsuit sharp, a lemon-colored silk blouse glowing under the lights. She took the stand with confidence and was sworn in quickly.

Barnes approached.

"Ms. Hopkins, please state your occupation for the record."

"I am the owner and lead broker at Hopkins Insurance Group in Pinecrest."

"Do you know the defendant, Patrice Wallen?"

"Yes. She and her husband, the late Russell Wallen, have been clients of ours for over ten years."

"Have you recently conducted any new business with the Wallens?"

"Yes. About three weeks before Mr. Wallen's death, Patrice came into our office to increase his life insurance coverage."

The gallery murmured again.

"And how much was the policy?"

"Five hundred thousand dollars, with Patrice listed as the sole beneficiary."

"Was Russell present for any of this?"

"No," Irene said. "I've only met him once or twice over the years. Patrice always handled their insurance matters."

"Did she also inquire about a life insurance policy for herself?"

"No. She said she had adequate coverage through her government employment."

"Did she give a reason for increasing Russell's policy?"

"Yes. She said Russell had recently had a medical exam, and they'd discussed the need for more coverage in case something happened to him."

"Did that raise any red flags for you?"

"No. It's common."

"With HIPAA regulations, how were you able to obtain medical records for Mr. Wallen?"

"We use a secure e-signature platform. The request form was signed through his personal email account."

"Is it possible Patrice could have signed that on his behalf?"

Irene hesitated. "It's possible… if she had access to his email. But our system treats an e-signature as valid authorization. It's standard industry practice."

Barnes nodded and stepped back. "No further questions."

Quentin was whispering with his client and after a few minutes he stood, adjusting his jacket slowly.

"Ms. Hopkins, you said you never spoke to Russell directly about this policy?"

"No, not me personally."

"Are you sure?"

Irene paused. "Let me check."

She flipped through her notes.

"Actually—yes. My assistant spoke to him by phone. He was having trouble with the e-signature, and she helped walk him through the process."

"So, it's reasonable to conclude that Russell knew a medical release was being signed?"

"Yes."

"And that would mean he was aware of the policy being initiated?"

"I would say that's likely, yes."

"No further questions."

Barnes was back on his feet. "Redirect, Your Honor?"

"Proceed."

"Ms. Hopkins, did the medical release request form specifically state the purpose as life insurance?"

"No," Irene said. "It's a standard form. Could be used for life insurance, auto claims, or liability claims—any reason we need access to medical information."

"So it's possible Russell signed the form not knowing it was for a new life insurance policy?"

"Yes, that is possible."

"No further questions."

Judge Nelson looked between the tables. "Counsel?"

Quentin stood. "No further questions, Your Honor."

"The witness is dismissed."

As Irene stepped down, the prosecution huddled in a quick, hushed discussion. Then Welsh rose and approached the bench.

"Your Honor, the State rests."

A wave of stillness fell over the courtroom. Then:

"We stand in recess until tomorrow morning. Mr. Stiles, be prepared to call your first witness at 9:00 a.m. sharp."

He gaveled once. Court adjourned.

Natalie sat frozen for a beat before typing furiously.

Trial Day Four – Morning Surprise

State Drops a Bombshell with Final Witness

Just when the courtroom thought the prosecution had rested its case, they called a surprise witness: Irene Hopkins, a respected insurance agent in Pinecrest.

Hopkins testified that just three weeks prior to Russell Wallen's death, a $500,000 life insurance policy was taken out in his name with Patrice Wallen as the sole beneficiary. She handled all documentation, and while she never spoke to Russell directly, her assistant did assist Russell by phone with the medical release signature.

The prosecution argued that the timing and beneficiary arrangement suggest possible premeditation. But Quentin Stiles was quick to highlight that Russell's signature was real, and the policy appears to have been signed with his knowledge.

Still, the seed has been planted: was this an act of foresight, or foresight with a motive?

Court resumes tomorrow at 9 a.m., with the defense finally preparing to present their case.

40

The conference room in Quentin's law office was usually a place of strategy, of deliberate planning and quiet confidence.

But tonight, it felt different.

A storm cloud of tension hovered over the long oak table as Quentin, Abigail, and Emily sat in stunned silence, still reeling from the curveball that had been launched into their case just hours before.

A steaming pot of coffee sat untouched in the center of the table. Paperwork lay scattered, highlighters abandoned.

Quentin rubbed his temples with both hands, then looked up.

"She forgot," he said, his voice low. "She *forgot* to tell us she took out a half-million-dollar life insurance policy on her husband… three weeks before she shot him."

Abigail exhaled sharply. "Not exactly the best look, heading into our first witness."

"No," Quentin replied. "It's not. That kind of omission makes it look like Patrice is being deceitful with her own counsel. And if the jury suspects that… we've lost before we even begin."

They all fell silent again, the gravity of the situation sinking deeper into the air.

Before Patrice had been taken back to the Asheville detention center that afternoon, Quentin had insisted on a brief private meeting with her in the courthouse interview room.

She had been sobbing the moment they walked in.

"I'm so sorry," she'd said over and over. "I didn't think about it—everything happened so fast. I wasn't trying to hide it. I forgot."

Quentin had kept his voice calm, but inside, the damage had already taken root.

Back at the office, Abigail pulled her notebook closer and flipped to a dog-eared page.

"I asked her about this," she said quietly. "As I always do. I go over a standard list of questions. We talked about life insurance—she told me both of them were covered through work. Small policies. Fifty, maybe a hundred thousand. Drafted out of their paychecks."

"She never said anything about going to Irene Hopkins?" Quentin asked.

Abigail shook her head. "Not once. And certainly nothing about a $500,000 policy."

Emily, who had been unusually quiet all evening, finally spoke. Her voice was hoarse.

"I can't stop thinking about that moment," she said, her eyes distant. "About her crying in that little room. And I keep asking myself… was she crying because she's truly sorry she forgot to tell us? Or because she got caught?"

A tear slipped down her cheek.

Quentin reached across the table and gently patted her hand.

"You feel like she betrayed you," he said softly.

Emily nodded. "I believed her. I still do, but… I'm just stunned. I'm sad. And now I'm questioning everything."

Abigail slumped back in her chair, pressing her palms to her eyes. "God, listen to us. We sound exactly like Paul Barnes. That smug look he had on his face today—I hated it. But he's going to hammer that insurance angle into the ground."

"He's not the only one," Quentin said grimly. "You can bet the Conrads are already feeding it to every whisper campaign in town. Joyce probably drafted her next Facebook post the second Irene stepped down."

The three of them sat in silence for a moment longer, then Quentin pushed back from the table and stood.

"Well," he said, voice steadying, "we don't have the luxury of lingering in this moment. We've got a client who's on trial for her life, and starting tomorrow, it's our turn."

He looked between them, eyes sharp.

"Our job isn't to judge her. It's to defend her. And we can't do that if we're sitting here wrapped in our own doubts."

He let the words settle.

"So," he added, "I need both of you to set those doubts down. Leave them right here on this table. Because when we walk into that courtroom tomorrow, we walk in unified. Rock solid."

Emily wiped her eyes and nodded.

Abigail looked down at her notes, then back up.

"I'm with you," she said quietly. "We'll give her the defense she deserves."

Quentin nodded once.

"Good. Now let's get to work."

He flipped open the defense's prep folder, turned to a clean page of his legal pad, and wrote the name at the top in bold, steady letters:

Lorinda Beaumont.

Natalie had barely said a word after arriving home that evening, still in a daze from the curveball the prosecution had thrown. The *Irene Hopkins* testimony had taken over her mind all evening—its timing, its tone, the sudden shift in courtroom energy. And now, with a glass of wine in hand and her legs tucked underneath her, she sat on the couch in the apartment above Valley Vogue, staring out the window at the darkened streetlights below.

Across from her, Baxter sat back in her worn leather armchair, still in his undershirt and jeans after changing out of his uniform. His beer sat untouched on the side table.

"So," Natalie finally said, breaking the silence, "do you think this changes anything Quentin had planned for the defense?"

Baxter rubbed his jaw, then leaned forward, resting his elbows on his knees.

"I wouldn't think so," he said. "He pretty much proved—at least for now—that Russell knew about the policy. That e-signature detail? That was important."

"Yeah, but…" Natalie sighed. "It still doesn't look good. Not the *policy*, necessarily—but the fact that Quentin didn't know about it? That it blindsided the defense team?"

Baxter nodded. "That's the part that'll be a black mark. Not the policy itself—jury might believe Russell agreed to it. But the fact that she didn't disclose it to her own lawyers?" He exhaled slowly. "That'll plant seeds of doubt. Makes Patrice look like she's hiding something, even if she's not."

Natalie frowned, swirling her wine.

"I watched Quentin the whole time during that testimony. He looked… angry. But not surprised angry. *Wounded* angry. Like he'd been punched in the gut by someone he trusted."

Baxter nodded again, slowly.

"I don't envy him," he said. "But he'll regroup. He'll figure out how to circumvent the setback."

"I just hate that it gives the prosecution momentum right before the defense starts their case," she muttered.

"You're not wrong," Baxter said. "Welsh and Barnes? They ended with a bang, and they know it."

Natalie tilted her head back against the cushions and sighed.

"I hope Quentin's ready for tomorrow."

Baxter looked at her, a small flicker of admiration in his expression.

"He will be. That man knows how to pull it together under pressure. And now? He's got something to prove—not just to the jury, but to himself."

41

By the time Judge Robert Nelson entered the courtroom and gaveled in the day's proceedings, the atmosphere was heavy with anticipation. Everyone in the room knew that Quentin would be calling his first witness, and the previous day's bombshell insurance testimony still lingered like a stain on the court's memory.

But Quentin's calm, confident demeanor didn't falter as he rose and said, "Your Honor, the defense calls Lorinda Beaumont to the stand."

A ripple of surprise moved through the gallery.

Lorinda, regal and composed, walked to the witness box with the grace of someone born into scrutiny—and long since mastered it. Her presence was elegant but grounded. She was not here to posture. She was here to speak truth.

Once sworn in, Quentin approached slowly.

"Mrs. Beaumont," he began, "can you please tell the court your profession?"

"I'm a registered nurse, currently not practicing full-time. At the time of the incident I'm about to discuss, I was working in the ER at Galen Valley Regional Medical Center."

"Were you on duty during an ER visit made by Patrice Wallen?"

"Yes. About two summers ago. She was brought in with visible trauma to her face—swelling, bruising, a split lip. Both of her eyes were red and puffy. She had difficulty speaking clearly because of the injuries."

"And what did she say caused the injuries?"

Lorinda took a long breath.

"She told us she fell in the garage, tripped on a box. But her injuries weren't consistent with that story. The pattern of bruising, the angle of the trauma—it looked more like she'd been hit. Repeatedly."

Gasps echoed softly from the gallery.

"Did anyone else treat her?"

"Yes. Dr. Clay Moreau. We both knew right away the story didn't match. We both begged her—begged her—to report the incident, to let us call law enforcement, to press charges. She refused."

Quentin stepped closer.

"Did she explain why?"

"She said she couldn't afford the fallout. That she would need to take at least a week off work so her coworkers wouldn't see her face. She said—and I quote—'There's no makeup strong enough to hide this.'"

Quentin's voice softened. "How did that moment impact you?"

Lorinda blinked rapidly but remained composed.

"It's haunted me. I've seen a lot of things in the ER, but the look in her eyes… that stays with you. She wasn't just hurt—she was broken. Trapped."

Quentin let the words land, then nodded and stepped back.

"No further questions, Your Honor."

District Attorney Tabitha Welsh stood with a sharpness that cracked through the courtroom's tension. Her stilettos clicked against the tile as she made her way to the stand, her eyes locked on Lorinda with icy precision.

"Mrs. Beaumont," she said, her voice edged with a smile, "how *convenient* that you remember so many details from a single ER visit two years ago. That must be quite the memory you have."

"I remember what matters," Lorinda said calmly.

Welsh nodded, pacing slowly.

"Tell me, do you often find yourself offering testimony in high-profile criminal trials?"

"No."

"Funny, because here you are," Welsh said, her voice rising just a notch, "taking the stand to defend a woman who shot her husband—coincidentally aligning yourself opposite your family's oldest rival."

Objection, Quentin barked.

"Sustained," said Judge Nelson. "Ms. Welsh, stay on topic."

Welsh continued.

"Your family has influence in this town. Your name is on the hospital wing. You're married into one of the most powerful families in Pinecrest County. Do you honestly expect this jury to believe that this isn't about you using your social standing to manipulate the outcome of this trial?"

Lorinda's eyes didn't flinch.

"I expect this jury to listen to the facts. Not to playground-level innuendo. Are we in middle school, Ms. Welsh, or a court of law?"

Gasps broke out. Even Judge Nelson had to hold back a cough that might've been a chuckle.

Welsh narrowed her eyes.

"So you're telling us this isn't about the Beaumonts versus the Conrads?"

Lorinda's voice remained poised. "It's about a woman who was beaten and refused to press charges out of fear. And now she's on trial for surviving."

"Isn't it possible she lied about the abuse to gain sympathy?"

"No," Lorinda snapped. "You can't fake injuries like the ones I treated. And you can't fake the *fear* I saw in her eyes."

"Or maybe," Welsh said, leaning forward, "she was just laying the groundwork for what she did on that trail."

"Enough," Judge Nelson said, rapping his gavel. "Counsel, approach."

As Quentin and Welsh stepped forward, the courtroom watched breathlessly. The judge leaned in and spoke softly, but firmly.

"Ms. Welsh, I'm going to caution you to keep this line of questioning focused on the matter at hand. We are not here to entertain social rivalries, family legacies, or personal vendettas. Is that clear?"

"Yes, Your Honor," Welsh said through clenched teeth.

Quentin returned to his seat, a slow grin spreading across his face. He didn't even need a redirect. The final impression of the witness was the DA being chastised by the judge.

Perfect.

"Mrs. Beaumont," Judge Nelson said. "You may step down."

Lorinda rose, dignified and poised, and returned to her seat behind the defense table.

The judge looked to the clock.

"We'll recess for lunch. Court resumes at one thirty."

Natalie, typing furiously from her fifth-row seat, paused just long enough to glance at Baxter, who gave her a subtle nod.

The tide had turned.

Back at Quentin's, the defense team gathered in the small conference room they'd converted into a war room for the duration of the trial. Stacks of folders, yellow legal pads, and half-drunk cups of coffee covered nearly every inch of the long table.

But now, for the first time in days, everyone was eating. The delivery guy from Grover's Deli had just left, and the room smelled of pastrami, grilled chicken, and tangy slaw.

Quentin unwrapped his sandwich with satisfaction and leaned back in his chair.

"Well," he said, taking a bite, "that was the best morning we've had since this trial started."

"No kidding," said Abigail, stabbing her fork into a side of potato salad. "Welsh lost her cool with that one. I've never seen her unravel like that."

"It's not like her," Abigail added thoughtfully. "I've watched her work for years. She's sharp. Controlled. She doesn't go for personal jabs—at least, she didn't use to."

"That's not Welsh running this case," Quentin replied as he wiped his hands on a napkin. "It's Joyce Conrad. She's driving the narrative from behind the scenes. She's the reason they're treating this like a family war."

"She's calling the shots?" Emily asked.

Quentin nodded. "Absolutely. And I'm just fine with it."

"Why?" Abigail asked.

"Because they'll lose," Quentin said, shrugging. "You let emotions run your trial, and you've already lost. You can't practice law with emotion. That's rule one."

Emily, quiet until now, set her sandwich down and looked at him. "But this afternoon, we're putting Patrice's mother on the stand, right?"

Quentin nodded.

"So… what exactly are we going to gain from that?" she asked.

Quentin smiled. "Emotion."

Emily blinked. "But you just said—"

"We can't be emotional," Quentin said, lifting his sandwich like a teaching aid. "Attorneys can't. Judges can't. But witnesses? Oh, they can pour it on."

Abigail chuckled as she sipped her sweet tea. "You'll get the jury to feel something again. Shift their energy."

"Exactly," Quentin said. "Patrice's mother doesn't need to be a powerhouse. She just needs to be honest. Vulnerable. That's what juries remember. Especially after Welsh came at Lorinda like a prosecutor in a political scandal. That contrast will serve us well."

Emily sat back in her chair, her lips pursed. "Sometimes I think I get this. Other times, I feel like I'm in a chess match blindfolded."

Abigail laughed. "That's why I always tell you—stay close to the master."

She pointed her fork at Quentin, who looked up from his sandwich, mock-flattered.

"Awww," he said. "Stop it, you'll make me blush."

"I'm serious," Abigail grinned. "Em, you've got instincts. And if you ever decide to take the plunge into law school, I'll be right there cheering you on."

Emily gave a half-smile, her eyes still shadowed from the night before, but a flicker of pride crossed her face.

"Let's just survive this case first."

They all laughed gently, the weight in the room lifting—if only for a moment.

Then Quentin pushed his plate aside, wiped his hands, and leaned forward, his tone shifting.

"Alright. Patrice's mom is up next. Let's go over her prep and make sure she stays in her lane. This has to be about her experience, not about Russell. We don't want her speculating—we want her remembering."

As he spoke, they opened new files and turned to fresh pages in their notepads.

The defense had drawn first blood.

Now, they had to keep momentum on their side.

42

The clock on the wall in Cassie's office ticked toward the bottom of the lunch hour, but she hadn't left her desk. She was elbow-deep in paperwork from the tax administration department, red-inking approval notes on reports when her cell phone buzzed against the polished wood surface.

Natalie.

Cassie smiled and answered. "Hey, Nat."

"Hi, bestie!" Natalie's voice came through bright and buzzing with energy.

Cassie laughed. "Well, someone's clearly enjoying the courtroom theatrics today."

"It was glorious," Natalie said, no hesitation. "Lorinda absolutely shredded Welsh. But my *favorite* part was when the judge stepped in and reprimanded her. You could hear a pin drop."

"I wish cameras were allowed in the courtroom," Cassie said, leaning back in her chair. "Seth texted me about it. Said Ridge Beaumont was furious over how the DA treated Lorinda."

"Can't blame him," Natalie replied. "She was composed but fierce—gave Welsh everything she deserved. And honestly? The jury *felt* it. You could see it in their faces."

"I'm glad to hear that," Cassie said. "Sounds like things are turning for Patrice."

"Definitely. So far, so good," Natalie agreed. "I'm looking forward to Angela's testimony this afternoon too. That should be—"

"Wait," Cassie interrupted, flipping a paper and glancing toward her door. "Angela's not testifying this afternoon. She's here—working

"

in her office. Emily told her she won't be called until tomorrow morning."

"Oh?" Natalie paused. "Well then... I wonder who Quentin is calling this afternoon?"

"No idea," Cassie said, "but whoever it is, I hope it keeps the momentum going."

"Same," Natalie said. "Baxter's heading my way now—I'm going to see what he thought about this morning."

"I'm sure he loved every second," Cassie said, smiling. "I'm thinking about picking up a bunch of pizzas tonight and having everyone over at the house."

"Count us in," Natalie said quickly. "We'll be there."

"Great," Cassie said, already mentally planning toppings and drink runs. "I'll text everyone. See you two tonight."

"You bet," Natalie said. "Talk soon, Cass."

Cassie hung up with a grin, her fingers already flying across the screen as she sent a group message out to Kathryn and Margaret—and of course one to Seth, who she needed to let know that they were hosting a pizza party.

There was something about gathering together after days like this.

It didn't solve anything. But it reminded them they weren't going through it alone.

When the courtroom reconvened for the afternoon session, the hum of conversation was low and subdued. After Lorinda Beaumont's firebrand testimony earlier, everyone seemed to sense a shift in tone—something more solemn was coming.

Quentin stood, buttoned his jacket, and addressed the court.

"Your Honor, the defense calls Valerie Austin to the stand."

A few surprised murmurs floated across the gallery as Patrice's mother rose from her seat and walked to the witness stand. Dressed in a pale lavender blouse and charcoal-gray slacks, her short curls neat and makeup minimal, Valerie Austin looked every inch a composed, dignified woman. But her eyes—lined with weariness and sorrow—told another story.

After she was sworn in, Quentin approached slowly.

"Mrs. Austin," he said gently, "can you tell the court how long you've known Russell Wallen?"

"Since Patrice brought him home to meet me," she replied softly. "That was... almost twenty years ago."

Quentin nodded. "And what was your impression of him then?"

"He was charming. Polite. Respectful," she said. "He brought flowers. Complimented my cooking. He was—" she paused "—a man any mother might be glad to see her daughter bring home."

Quentin waited a beat.

"And over the years, did that impression change?"

Valerie looked down at her hands for a moment. "Not at first. But things... began to shift. Patrice started coming around less. When she did, she was quieter. Seemed tired. Nervous."

"Did you ever suspect anything was wrong?"

"I suspected," Valerie admitted, her voice trembling. "But I didn't want to believe it. I told myself it was the stress of her job. Politics. Marriage. Life. I looked away."

Quentin's voice softened. "Did you ever witness anything firsthand?"

"No," she said. "But there were times—times I saw bruises she blamed on clumsiness. Times she flinched when someone moved too fast. Times she showed up late to dinners and left early, barely speaking."

"And what did you do with those suspicions?"

Valerie's voice cracked. "I buried them. I didn't ask. I didn't push. I didn't want to see what was right in front of me. I was afraid of what it would mean... for her. For me."

There was a hush in the courtroom.

"Did you speak with Patrice after her arrest?" Quentin asked.

"Yes. A few days ago," Valerie said, nodding. "They let me see her in the detention center. I sat with her in a little room and I told her… I was sorry. For not seeing it. For not helping her. For pushing it aside. I asked her to forgive me."

"And what did she say?"

"She pressed her hand to the glass partition where my hand was," Valerie said, her voice breaking now. "And she said, 'Mama, I forgive you.' And that she still loved me."

Sniffles echoed from the gallery. A tissue was passed down one of the benches. Even several jurors had glossy eyes.

Quentin let the silence stretch a moment before stepping back.

"No further questions, Your Honor."

He returned to the defense table.

Judge Nelson looked to the prosecution table. "Cross-examination?"

Tabitha Welsh, still recovering from the morning's reprimand, stood but immediately shook her head. "The State has no questions for this witness."

"Very well," Judge Nelson said. "Mrs. Austin, thank you. You may step down."

As Valerie walked to take her seat behind Patrice, a long exhale passed through the courtroom like the last gust of wind before the calm.

The judge glanced at the clock.

"This court will recess until tomorrow morning. We will resume at 9 AM."

The gavel fell.

Natalie closed her laptop, her fingers having flown over the keys for the last few minutes of Valerie's testimony. She gave the summary one last glance before clicking Post.

Trial Day Four – Afternoon Session Summary

The defense called Valerie Austin, mother of Patrice Wallen, to the stand this afternoon. Her testimony, soft-spoken but deeply emotional, painted a haunting portrait of a mother's guilt and a daughter's quiet suffering.

Valerie recounted years of subtle signs that something was wrong, and her decision to look the other way. She described her recent visit to Patrice in detention, a conversation marked by apology and forgiveness.

The State declined to cross-examine.

If this trial has taught us anything, it's that truth doesn't always shout—it sometimes whispers. And today, that whisper came from a mother who finally saw what was always there.

Court resumes tomorrow. Stay tuned.

She clicked off her screen and slid the laptop into her bag.

Baxter was waiting by the elevator, hands in his pockets.

"You ready?" he asked with a slight smile.

Natalie nodded, a glint of anticipation in her eyes.

"Let's go eat pizza and decompress. I think Cassie's going to need two bottles of wine for this one."

43

The smell of melted cheese and fresh garlic filled the Dixon house as Seth laid the last box of pizza on the long kitchen island. Plates were stacked, drinks chilled, and everyone had been told to wear comfortable clothes—no politics, no pressure, just friends.

The lights were warm and dim, candles flickering across the dining room table and into the adjacent living space where laughter was already starting to build.

"Alright," Seth announced, clapping his hands once, "you've got choices—pepperoni, veggie, supreme, barbecue chicken, and… someone's brave enough to ask for pineapple."

"That would be me," Kathryn said, raising her hand with a smile. "I like chaos on a crust."

"Blasphemy," Bronte grumbled from the couch. "Fruit doesn't belong on pizza. Or stew. Or anywhere it shouldn't be."

"You're just mad it's not elk meat," Margaret teased, sipping her iced tea.

Cassie chuckled, sliding into a chair beside Natalie, who had just arrived with Baxter, both of them still glowing from the courtroom drama earlier.

"So," Cassie said, folding her napkin, "let's talk about it. All of it."

"You mean the state's character parade followed by the unraveling of their narrative?" Natalie said.

"Exactly that."

Bronte, seated with a full plate and his feet propped up, looked visibly agitated. "Still stewin' over how Lorinda was treated. That woman doesn't have a bone of ill intent in her whole body. And they tried to twist her into some manipulative socialite."

"She handled it brilliantly," Natalie said, nodding. "Did you see the way she stayed calm? And that 'are we in middle school or a courtroom' line? That was gold."

"I'm proud of her," Bronte said, quieter now. "But I hate that she had to go through it. She's got a soft heart."

Margaret leaned forward, her voice thoughtful. "We all need to remember—Joyce Conrad is pulling the strings. Don't let Tabitha Welsh fool you. This isn't just a murder trial. This is a show of power by the Conrad family, and it's meant to send a message."

"Backfiring beautifully," Baxter said, biting into a slice.

"I agree," Margaret continued. "But make no mistake: if the state loses this case, it won't just be a loss for the prosecution—it'll be a crack in the Conrad legal empire. And that crack might just spread."

"Well," Cassie said, raising her water glass, "that legal network has operated unchecked for too long. Look what it did to Galen Valley. We're still clawing our way out of that corruption."

"I do see the light at the end of the tunnel though," Margaret added.

Kathryn chimed in. "Speaking of that light… Angela's testimony tomorrow might finally push this into daylight. Under oath, there's a lot she is going to say that's going to make some people *very* nervous. She'll look good doing it too, I know because I picked out her outfit."

Everyone laughed as Baxter nodded and said, "The state and federal investigators are both going to be in the courtroom tomorrow."

"They are?" Natalie asked, blinking.

"Yep," Baxter confirmed. "They've been in touch with the state auditor's office. Out of respect for the trial, they're holding off on official moves, but I wouldn't be surprised if I'm asked to serve grand jury indictments within the week."

Cassie took a deep breath. "Angela has prepared her report. And tomorrow she will testify to the facts—everything Russell was hiding, the shady budgeting, and all the names that pop up alongside his."

A moment of silence passed as everyone took that in.

Kathryn broke it with a dramatic sigh. "The drama never ends."

The conversation slowly drifted toward less intense topics—Natalie's skyrocketing blog traffic, Kathryn's latest shipment of fall scarves that Bronte had to carry upstairs like "a mountain mule," and Seth's disaster of a DIY bathroom project that had cost them an entire weekend and most of his dignity.

Laughter rang out, the kind that came easily when people knew they were among friends.

As the evening wore on and the pizza boxes thinned out, Bronte stood and stretched with a groan.

"Well," he said, "hate to be the party pooper, but it's past my bedtime."

"Of course it is," Kathryn teased, standing and throwing an arm around his waist. "The sun went down four hours ago. Bronte's usually asleep by seven. I appreciate him staying out so late to party with us tonight."

He gave her a rare grin and hugged her back. "Alright, enough of that, woman. Take me home."

Everyone laughed as they said their goodbyes, hugging and waving and promising to regroup in a few days.

Cassie stood at the door with Seth, arms around each other, watching as their friends disappeared into the night.

"You know," she said softly, "I think we're going to be alright."

Seth kissed her temple. "Of course we are."

44

The courtroom was unusually still as Angela Wilkes stepped into the witness box.

Dressed in a deep burgundy blazer over a chic black sheath dress with her dark curls pinned back neatly, she gave off the poised energy of someone who had come not to speculate—but to testify. Her eyes swept the courtroom only once before settling on Quentin, who rose from the defense table with a calm, focused expression.

After she was sworn in, Quentin approached slowly, tapping the corner of his legal pad with the end of his pen.

"Ms. Wilkes," he began, "please state your current position for the court."

"I'm the acting finance director for the Town of Galen Valley."

"And how long have you held that role?"

"Since the death of Russell Wallen. I was his assistant prior to that."

Quentin nodded. "Now, Ms. Wilkes, can you describe what you discovered upon assuming that role?"

Angela took a breath, steadying herself.

"Yes. In the days immediately following Mr. Wallen's death, I began a routine review of the office's files—budget reports, grant applications, infrastructure proposals. During that review, I also started looking over the documentation that the investigators had found inside a locked drawer in Mr. Wallen's office."

"Did the SBI indicate they had reviewed the documents as well?"

"The SBI had conducted a surface review of the documents in the office and assumed they were local government documentation—standard budgetary information."

"But that wasn't the case."

Angela leaned forward slightly.

"No. What was inside that drawer had nothing to do with the Town of Galen Valley. It was related to a separate shell corporation, one that appeared to be laundering taxpayer dollars through a series of suspicious accounts and fictitious vendors."

A gasp echoed from somewhere in the gallery.

Quentin kept his expression neutral. "Can you explain how the laundering worked?"

Angela nodded. "Federal infrastructure funds allocated to Galen Valley were being redirected through this shell entity under the pretense of subcontracts. On paper, it looked like the funds were being used for engineering consultants, materials, even site inspections. But those companies didn't exist. It was all fabricated—documents, invoices, checks."

"And whose name was on these documents?"

Angela picked up a folder from the table beside her and opened it.

"There were three names that appeared repeatedly across every document, account registration, and financial transaction log: Russell Wallen, Sandra Greer, and Veronica Altameda."

Quentin paused. "Were any of these documents signed by Patrice Wallen?"

"No."

"Did her name appear in any of the records?"

"No. Not once."

Quentin let that settle into the room like dust after an explosion.

"Did you immediately report your findings?"

"Yes. I informed Mayor Dixon within twenty-four hours. We began an internal review to verify the scope of the documents and ensure that no one else from the finance department had any involvement."

"And what was the result of that review?"

Angela took a deep breath.

"We confirmed that the shell entity was a cleverly disguised laundering system operating alongside the real budgetary processes of the town. Russell had been skimming and redirecting funds without oversight. It was so well-integrated that only a detailed line-by-line audit revealed the discrepancies."

"Was this happening during the time Mr. Wallen was testifying against Denise Carrow?"

"Yes. In fact, most of the backdated records begin in that same timeframe. While he was presenting himself as a whistleblower… he was quietly engaging in his own scheme."

Quentin turned toward the jury. "Just so we're clear—Russell Wallen was simultaneously testifying to help expose corruption in Galen Valley… while continuing his own financial fraud behind the scenes?"

Angela nodded gravely. "That is correct."

He stepped away, giving the courtroom a full view of the witness.

"One final question," he said. "Have you turned over this information to the appropriate state agencies?"

"Yes. The State Auditor's Office has full copies of the documents. I have also prepared additional files for potential federal review. They are aware of the findings but, as I understand it, are waiting until the trial concludes before taking official action."

"No further questions, Your Honor."

Quentin returned to his table.

The silence that followed was thick. The kind of silence that didn't just represent shock—it represented recalculation. All the courtroom's assumptions about Russell Wallen, the so-called loyal public servant, were unraveling by the minute.

Judge Nelson looked to the prosecution table.

"Ms. Welsh? Mr. Barnes?"

Paul Barnes rose. "We reserve the right to recall the witness, Your Honor, but we have no immediate questions."

Angela remained composed as she was dismissed.

As she walked past the defense table, she made brief eye contact with Patrice, who mouthed, thank you.

Angela gave the slightest nod in return.

And just like that, the defense's narrative shifted from self-defense to justified revelation—not just about abuse, but about a man who had deceived an entire town and nearly taken his wife down with him.

The tide, once again, was turning.

45

The door to the small conference room slammed shut harder than necessary, shaking the coffee mugs resting on the counter along the back wall.

Joyce, heels clicking across the tile, whirled on Tabitha and Paul with a fury that had been bubbling since the moment Angela Wilkes stepped down from the witness stand.

"I told you this would happen," Joyce hissed, her manicured finger pointed like a dagger. "I told you the defense would twist this financial nonsense into a sideshow. That woman just accused my son of *stealing* from the town he helped rebuild!"

Paul stayed seated, leafing through a printed copy of the ledgers Angela had turned over to the auditor. "We knew these documents existed, Mrs. Conrad. That's why we reserved the right to recall her later."

"You let her say those things about my son *unopposed!*"

Welsh stood calmly and folded her arms. "She stated facts, Joyce. Hard to argue with files that bear his signature."

"She was *his assistant's assistant*—you're telling me a mid-level bookkeeper gets to assassinate my son's reputation while the two of you just sit there?"

"She's the acting finance director," Paul said flatly. "And she didn't assassinate anything. She gave sworn testimony about records your son kept locked in his office."

Joyce's face flushed with indignation. "This is an ambush. Russell can't defend himself. And that *woman*—that Patrice—is going to walk free if you keep letting that sleazy defense attorney run the show."

196

Welsh's tone sharpened. "We're not amateurs, Mrs. Conrad. We have the same documentation Angela Wilkes has. We've been aware of it since the defense turned it over. And we have a plan."

Joyce narrowed her eyes. "What plan?"

"We'll address it in our rebuttal case," Paul said, sliding the documents into a folder. "For now, we let the defense paint their picture. But when we recall Angela—and we will—we'll shift the narrative. Her testimony raises just as many questions as it answers."

"Like how she just 'happened' to find the files after the agents didn't?" Joyce spat. "Sounds more like she's covering her own tracks to me."

Welsh sighed. "We'll address that. But we need to stay focused. Losing our composure now won't help the case."

Joyce gave them both a steely glare. "I want her credibility destroyed. Her career, her license—whatever it takes. You understand me?"

Welsh stared at her for a long moment.

"We'll do our job, Mrs. Conrad," she said coolly. "I suggest you let us."

Joyce turned on her heel and stormed out of the room, her designer purse slapping against her side like a gavel of its own.

Published: 3:02 p.m.

The Ledger That Changed Everything

I've sat in courtrooms before and witnessed pivotal moments—twists in the narrative that send ripples across the case and beyond. But nothing has struck quite as deeply as what happened today in the courtroom during Angela Wilke's testimony.

As many of you now know, Angela, the acting finance director for the Town of Galen Valley, took the stand this morning and presented a stunning revelation: that Russell Wallen, beloved longtime finance director and the very man who helped expose former mayor Denise Carrow's corruption, had been engaging in a scheme of his own—*laundering taxpayer funds* through a shell corporation while serving in his trusted position.

Let that sink in. The man hailed as a public servant was running a separate, secret operation behind closed drawers—literally.

Angela testified that she discovered this scheme only after stepping into Russell's role following his death. She described obtaining documentation from the investigators that they assumed were Galen Valley financial ledgers and finding a paper trail that led not to the town's operating accounts, but to fake vendors, fabricated projects, and diverted funds.

Perhaps the most damning moment of her testimony came when she was asked whose names appeared across the shell corporation's documents. She responded clearly and unequivocally:

- Russell Wallen

- Sandra Greer

- Veronica Altameda

Notably absent from that list? Patrice Wallen.

There are still questions, of course. Why didn't Russell's activities surface sooner? Who else knew? What happens next?

The State Auditor's Office is reportedly aware and monitoring developments. It is likely this information will lead to further investigations—possibly indictments—when this trial concludes.

But today, one thing became undeniably clear:

The image of Russell Wallen as a flawless civic hero has cracked.

And for the jurors sitting in that room, watching Patrice Wallen's trial unfold—those cracks might be enough to see her not just as a defendant, but as a woman caught in the wake of a very different truth.

Stay tuned. Tomorrow promises even more revelations.

46

The courtroom was packed.

The energy had shifted after Angela Wilkes' financial testimony the day before, and everyone knew the defense wasn't done with her yet. The media presence outside had doubled. Reporters loitered in hallways. Blog hits were climbing. Even the jurors looked more alert.

Quentin rose from the defense table as soon as Judge Robert Nelson gaveled the morning session open.

"Your Honor," he said smoothly, "the defense would like to recall Angela Wilkes to the stand."

Angela stepped forward again, calm and composed in a cream suit with a dusty rose blouse, her expression unreadable. Once she was reminded she was still under oath, Quentin approached slowly, the faintest flicker of momentum in his stride.

"Ms. Wilkes," he said, "can you tell the court where you were approximately three days ago, during the morning hours?"

"I was at Town Hall, working in my office," she replied. "Mayor Dixon and I were reviewing the final batch of audit documentation for submission to the state."

"Did anyone unexpected come to visit you that morning?"

"Yes. A man named Fergus Greer."

Quentin nodded. "And for the record, who is Mr. Fergus Greer?"

"He is the ex-husband of Sandra Greer, who was communications director during Denise Carrow's administration. Sandra is now retired."

"And why did Mr. Greer come to see you?"

Angela's voice grew more measured. "He said he wanted to make sure he didn't go down with his ex-wife. That he had stayed silent for too long, but he didn't want to carry guilt for something he didn't do. He said he had reason to believe that Sandra Greer and Russell Wallen were having an affair."

The ripple that moved through the gallery was instant—shocked murmurs, exchanged glances, even a dropped pen from one of the jurors.

Angela continued. "Mr. Greer said he had followed Sandra on multiple occasions when she claimed she was out of town with friends. But instead, he saw her meeting with Mr. Wallen at two separate locations—a beach house in Savannah, and a penthouse in Buckhead. He claimed both properties were owned by Joyce Conrad and her husband."

At the mention of her name, Joyce lurched forward in her seat behind the prosecution table.

"Objection!" Paul Barnes called from his chair, but the judge waved it off.

"I'll allow it," Judge Nelson said, "Continue, Ms. Wilkes."

Angela remained steady.

"He said he confronted Sandra and threatened to expose them. She begged him not to ruin her career and promised it was over. But he suspected it continued. He believed Russell had been physically abusive to Sandra as well. He claimed to have photographs."

At that moment, Patrice Wallen's hand flew to her mouth. She turned toward her attorney, stunned.

And then it happened.

Joyce Conrad shot to her feet.

"You liar!" she screamed, pointing a trembling finger at Angela. "You disgusting little liar! How *dare* you drag my family through the mud! How *dare* you lie about my son!"

Gasps erupted across the courtroom.

"Mrs. Conrad!" Judge Nelson called out, banging his gavel.

Tabitha Welsh and Paul Barnes immediately rushed to calm her, but Joyce kept yelling.

"You think this'll save her?" she shouted, spinning toward the defense table. "You think dragging my son through the dirt is going to make *that woman* look innocent?"

She jabbed her finger at Patrice. "You gold-digging little witch! You killed him, and now you're trying to stain his name!"

"Mrs. Conrad!" Judge Nelson thundered. "You are out of order! Bailiff!"

Baxter, who had already stepped forward, moved quickly to intervene. He gently, but firmly, grabbed Joyce's elbow as her husband, Lawrence, stood and tried to calm her with a firm hand on her shoulder.

"I will not sit here while you defame my son!" Joyce shrieked as Baxter guided her toward the courtroom doors. "This trial is a mockery! A disgrace!"

"Escort both Mr. and Mrs. Conrad out of the courtroom," Judge Nelson ordered. "We are in recess for one hour."

He slammed the gavel again before turning toward the stunned prosecution table.

"I do not want to be the one who tells the *mother of the deceased victim* that she's banned from her own son's trial—but I *will* do so if I must. We must maintain order in this courtroom. I understand emotions are high, and this is difficult to hear. But I will *not* allow this trial to become a spectacle. Am I understood?"

"Clearly, Your Honor," Tabitha Welsh replied tightly, nodding. "We will ensure Mrs. Conrad remains calm during the remainder of this trial."

The gavel fell once more.

"Court is in recess."

Published: 11:22 a.m.

Courtroom Eruption: The Morning the Gallery Exploded

If you've been following this trial, you've likely come to expect the unexpected. But this morning, the courtroom was rocked by an explosive revelation—and an even more explosive reaction.

Angela Wilkes returned to the stand and testified under oath that a man named Fergus Greer, ex-husband of Sandra Greer, came to Town Hall just three days ago to confess to knowing about an affair between Sandra and Russell Wallen. According to Ms. Wilkes, Fergus provided specific details, including properties they allegedly used for their secret meetings—properties tied to none other than Joyce Conrad and her husband.

The courtroom didn't just gasp. It erupted.

Joyce Conrad stood up and began yelling at Angela from the gallery. Her words were sharp, angry, and directed not just at the witness, but at the defense—and at Patrice herself. The judge tried to restore order but ultimately had to ask Sheriff Baxter Ross to remove Mrs. Conrad and her husband from the courtroom.

Judge Nelson has recessed court for an hour.

What does this mean for the case? What will happen when the courtroom reconvenes? All I know is this: if anyone thought this trial had already peaked in drama, think again.

Stay with me. I'll be live-blogging this afternoon's session. Things are only heating up.

47

The interview room off the back hallway of the courthouse was small, quiet, and dimly lit. The hum of the air conditioning filled the silence as Patrice sat hunched forward on the edge of her chair, hands clasped tightly in her lap.

Quentin sat across from her, elbows on the table, fingers laced, watching her carefully. Emily and Abigail stood just behind him, giving Patrice space but ready to step in if needed.

She hadn't said a word since they entered the room.

Her lips were slightly parted, her breathing shallow.

Finally, Quentin spoke. "You okay?"

Patrice blinked slowly, her voice barely above a whisper. "Did that really just happen?"

Quentin nodded. "It did."

"She—" Patrice paused, trying to form the thought. "Joyce… she said I killed him and then dragged his name through the mud."

"She lost control," Abigail said gently. "It was a meltdown."

"She didn't just call me a liar," Patrice murmured, eyes glassy. "She called me… a gold-digging witch. In front of everyone."

Quentin leaned forward. "What people saw today wasn't *your* shame, Patrice. It was hers."

"She's grieving," Emily offered quietly. "But that doesn't excuse it."

Patrice looked at Quentin. "Is the jury going to believe any of this? That Russell had an affair? That he hit Sandra too? That he was laundering money?"

Quentin's voice was calm but resolute. "They already believe some of it. The documents speak for themselves. The rest? We're building

204

piece by piece. What Angela said today? It was powerful. You saw the courtroom shift."

Patrice nodded, though slowly. "It's just... hearing it aloud. That he cheated. That his name is tied to *all of this*... I didn't know. I didn't know any of it. And still, I stayed."

Abigail stepped forward and put a hand on Patrice's shoulder. "A lot of women stay, Patrice. That doesn't make you weak. It makes you human."

Patrice's eyes filled, and she nodded, wiping the corner of her eye.

Quentin stood. "Let's take this hour. We need to all decompress from what just took place then we will go back in and finish up with Fergus Greer's testimony. Do you think you can handle this?"

Patrice took a long breath and straightened her spine. "Okay," she said. "Okay."

Joyce paced the private conference room like a caged animal. Her husband, Lawrence, sat silently in a chair, one hand resting on a copy of the trial docket.

Tabitha entered first, followed by Paul, both of them far less composed than usual.

Tabitha shut the door with deliberate force.

"Joyce," she began, "we need to talk. And I'm going to be very direct."

Joyce turned on her heel. "Don't start with me, Tabitha. You let that woman sit up there and accuse my son of being an abuser *and* a cheater. What do you expect me to do—sit there with my pearls and clutch them politely?"

"We expect you to follow the rules of a court of law," Paul cut in sharply. "What happened in that courtroom was completely out of line."

Joyce glared at him. "She's lying. All of them are."

"We don't know that," Tabitha said firmly. "And whether she is or isn't, that's not your decision to make. The court is where the facts are tested—not in a shouting match in front of the jury."

"I was defending my son!"

"You were compromising the very case meant to honor him," Paul shot back. "You do understand that if you keep this up, the judge can declare a mistrial?"

Joyce paled, but her lips pressed into a tight line.

Lawrence finally spoke, his voice low. "Joyce, they're right."

She stared at him. "Excuse me?"

He sighed. "I didn't want to say it in front of everyone, but you've crossed a line. If the judge bars us from the courtroom, what kind of message does that send? You're giving them ammunition."

Tabitha softened her tone, just slightly. "We're not saying don't grieve. But this isn't a private mourning—this is a public trial. Every time you lose control, it reflects on the prosecution."

Joyce didn't respond. Her eyes shimmered, but no tears fell.

Paul spoke again, quieter now. "The judge was generous today. But if it happens again, we won't be able to stop what comes next."

Joyce looked down, her jaw clenching. "Fine," she whispered.

"We're holding you to that," Tabitha said. "We *have to*."

The room fell silent. Tense. Fragile.

Finally, Joyce turned toward the door. "I need a moment."

She left without waiting for acknowledgment, her heels clicking down the hallway with far less confidence than before.

Lawrence stood slowly and gave the prosecutors a small, apologetic nod. "I'll make sure she keeps it together."

"Please do," Paul said. "The trial isn't over yet."

The courtroom was still tense from the earlier outburst as the afternoon session resumed. The bailiff closed the heavy double doors behind the last juror, and Judge Nelson entered from his chambers with a more stern-than-usual expression.

Quentin rose confidently, adjusting his jacket as he stepped toward the center of the courtroom.

"The defense calls Fergus Greer to the stand."

A ripple passed through the gallery.

Immediately, Tabitha stood. "Objection, Your Honor! This is a last-minute witness the prosecution was given no notice of. We have received no discovery on this individual or any alleged testimony he might provide."

The judge's brow creased as he looked down at the docket. "Counsel, approach."

Quentin picked up two manila envelopes from his table and met Tabitha and Paul Barnes at the bench.

Judge Nelson lowered his voice. "Explain."

"Your Honor," Quentin said evenly, offering an envelope to the judge and another to Tabitha, "Mr. Fergus Greer came to see me just a few days ago. As your honor knows, Ms. Wilkes testified to his visit at Town Hall. At the time, he said he had documentation—photographs—that he kept in a safety deposit box."

"And you're just now getting them?" Tabitha asked sharply.

"This morning," Quentin confirmed. "He was finally able to access the box, and he brought them directly to me. I'm handing them over to the court and prosecution immediately upon receipt. I'm not hiding anything."

Tabitha opened the envelope in front of her and flipped through the glossy, time-stamped photos. Her face hardened.

The judge reviewed the materials in his own envelope. "Ms. Welsh, Ms. Wilkes did testify to this visit. If the photos and Greer's testimony support her account, it would be prejudicial to deny the jury that corroboration."

Tabitha pursed her lips. "Your Honor, I just ask that we be allowed to reserve a full cross-examination once we've had time to properly review the photos and question the authenticity."

"Noted," the judge said. He glanced at Quentin. "You'll make Mr. Greer available should the prosecution wish to recall him?"

"Of course," Quentin replied.

"Then I'll allow it."

Tabitha gave Paul a tight look, one that said everything without a word: *This is not going well.*

They returned to their seats, and the judge banged his gavel once.

"Proceed, Mr. Stiles."

Quentin turned toward the gallery doors just as Fergus Greer was led into the courtroom by a bailiff. He was a wiry man in his early fifties, weathered but sharp-eyed, dressed in a worn blazer that hung a little too loose on his frame.

He was sworn in and took his place at the stand.

Quentin approached with the calm precision of someone who knew this was a pivotal moment.

"Mr. Greer, thank you for joining us. Please state your name for the court."

"Fergus Greer."

"And you are the ex-husband of Sandra Greer, formerly the communications director under Denise Carrow's administration?"

"That's correct."

Quentin nodded. "Can you tell the court why you came to see Angela Wilkes and Mayor Cassie Dixon a few days ago?"

Fergus took a breath. "Because I didn't want to carry it anymore. I've known about Sandra's affair with Russell Wallen for years. And I couldn't sit back while the woman he abused was on trial for his death—when no one knew what kind of man he really was."

Quentin let the courtroom absorb that.

"And today, you turned over photographic evidence to support that claim?"

Fergus nodded. "Yes. I kept them in a safety deposit box because, frankly, I was scared. Russell was connected. So was Sandra. I didn't want to blow up their reputations. But I followed her a few times when she lied about going out of town with friends. Instead, I caught her meeting Russell—once at a beach house in Savannah, and another time at a penthouse in Buckhead."

Quentin picked up one of the photos from the defense table and held it up for the jury.

"This is one of the images you took?"

"Yes. Date-stamped. That's them walking into the house together."

"Were you aware that both properties were owned by Joyce and Lawrence Conrad?"

"Yes," Fergus said, his voice cool. "I looked up the property records myself."

Quentin paused. "Did you ever confront Sandra?"

"I did. She swore it was over. Said it had just been a fling. I didn't believe her."

"And were there any signs of abuse?"

Fergus's expression darkened. "She came home from one of those weekends with a bruise on her ribcage. Said she fell in the shower. I didn't believe her. That bruise looked like someone had kicked her."

Quentin turned to the judge. "I'll move to enter the photographs and supporting documentation into evidence."

"Entered," Judge Nelson said.

Quentin returned to his table.

The room was dead quiet.

"Your witness," he said, turning toward the prosecution.

Tabitha stood slowly. "We reserve full cross for a later date, Your Honor. We will need time to authenticate the images and review the documents."

"Understood," said the judge.

As Fergus was dismissed, Quentin could feel the weight in the room shift again.

The perfect image of Russell Wallen was coming undone.

Piece by piece.

48

The Unraveling: What Fergus Greer Just Did to This Trial

Today in court, a name we hadn't yet heard in testimony—Fergus Greer—took the stand and changed the game.

Mr. Greer, the ex-husband of Sandra Greer, testified under oath that Sandra was involved in a long-term affair with Russell Wallen, the alleged victim in this case.

But that wasn't all.

Fergus came with photographic evidence—time-stamped pictures retrieved from his safety deposit box just this morning. These images place Russell and Sandra together at private properties reportedly owned by Joyce and Lawrence Conrad—yes, *those* Conrads, the same family leading the charge to convict Patrice Wallen.

His words were calm, but his message was a shockwave: the Russell Wallen everyone thought they knew may have been hiding much more than just an affair. Mr. Greer also mentioned suspected abuse… and financial ties that we now know align with other testimony in this case.

If this trial was already complicated, it just turned inside out.

Questions now swirl:

Did Russell's family know about the affair?

Were the properties used without their knowledge—or with it?

And what else might Sandra Greer be hiding?

The courtroom sat stunned as Judge Nelson entered the photos into evidence, over the prosecution's objection. I'm still processing it all.

So is the jury. But one thing is clear: the story of Russell Wallen is no longer simple—and this trial is far from over.

The thick envelope of photographs sat open on the conference table, its contents now fanned out across the surface like the broken pieces of a mirror.

Tabitha leaned over one image, her brow furrowed.

It showed Russell Wallen and Sandra Greer seated at an upscale restaurant—arms touching, mid-laugh. Across the table, clearly captured in the background, sat Joyce and Lawrence Conrad, wine glasses raised, engaged in cheerful conversation.

Paul pushed another photo forward. This one was at the Buckhead penthouse, dated six months earlier. Joyce again appeared in the frame, this time stepping off the elevator with Sandra, both carrying designer shopping bags.

Joyce sat across from them now in the same conference room, her face pale but resolute.

Lawrence sat beside her, his mouth drawn in a thin line, his eyes unreadable.

"Care to explain these?" Tabitha asked, her voice clipped but steady.

Joyce gave the smallest shrug. "Shopping trips. Business dinners. Sandra was part of the financial advisory team. So was Russell."

Paul didn't look up from the photo. "So you were aware of their relationship?"

Joyce's chin lifted. "They were colleagues."

"And the Buckhead property?" Tabitha pressed. "Owned by you and your husband?"

"Yes. It was available to family and trusted associates."

"And you had *no* idea that Russell and Sandra were having an affair there?"

Joyce bristled. "That's a *stretch,* and you know it."

Tabitha's tone sharpened. "We also now know those properties may have been used to facilitate the laundering of public funds through shell corporations. Funds Angela Wilkes says trace directly back to Russell, Sandra, and Veronica Altameda."

Paul added, "You're listed as co-owner of both properties."

Joyce turned to Lawrence, who still hadn't said a word.

"Lawrence, say something," she snapped.

But Lawrence simply rubbed his temple and looked at Tabitha. "What are you suggesting?"

"We're not suggesting anything—yet," Tabitha said. "But I'd be negligent not to ask: *Did either of you know what Russell and Sandra were doing with those funds?* Were you helping them move money through those properties?"

Joyce stood abruptly. "This is a witch hunt."

"No," Tabitha said coldly. "This is a trial. And these questions will come up again—especially if federal charges follow."

Joyce opened her mouth but paused.

Lawrence finally stood, too. "You'll get no more from us today."

Tabitha crossed her arms. "Then I suggest you prepare yourselves. Because this courtroom isn't finished with the Wallens—or the Conrads."

49

The courtroom was at capacity as Judge Nelson gaveled in. The buzz from yesterday's testimony had not dissipated; if anything, the air was thicker with anticipation.

Quentin stood as soon as the judge nodded toward the defense.

"The defense calls Angela Wilkes back to the stand for redirect, Your Honor."

Angela returned to the stand, her face composed but tired. She adjusted the mic slightly and folded her hands in her lap, waiting.

Quentin approached calmly, his voice measured and purposeful.

"Ms. Wilkes, earlier this week you testified that upon stepping into your role as acting finance director, you discovered documents that led you to uncover a shell corporation used to redirect public funds—specifically infrastructure grant money—away from legitimate town projects and into accounts affiliated with Russell Wallen, Sandra Greer, and Veronica Altameda. Is that correct?"

"Yes," Angela replied. "That is correct."

"Did you take any immediate steps upon making that discovery?"

"Yes. I brought the documents to Mayor Dixon and initiated an internal investigation. We cross-referenced grant allocations, vendor records, and budget trails going back nearly four years."

"Were these findings shared with anyone else?"

Angela nodded. "We compiled everything and submitted a full report to the State Auditor's Office, including spreadsheets, scanned invoices, and original hardcopy signatures from Russell Wallen."

Quentin handed a thick binder to the court clerk. "Your Honor, this is a certified copy of the report submitted to the auditor. May we enter it into evidence?"

"Admitted," said Judge Nelson.

Quentin turned back to Angela. "Did Patrice Wallen appear anywhere in that report?"

"No," Angela said firmly. "I never found a single reference to Patrice in any of the records. Not in payment authorizations, vendor documents, account trails—nothing."

Quentin nodded. "And in your professional opinion, Ms. Wilkes, based on what you've uncovered and what's been presented in court—was Russell Wallen operating a second, concealed financial scheme that directly contradicts his public image?"

Angela hesitated only for a second before answering.

"Yes. Without a doubt."

"No further questions, Your Honor."

As Quentin returned to the defense table, Tabitha was already rising, legal pad in hand, eyes cold and calculating.

She approached the witness stand slowly.

"Ms. Wilkes," she began, "you've testified at length about a discovery made after Russell Wallen's death. And yet, isn't it true that prior to becoming acting finance director, you worked in the finance office for over three years?"

"Yes," Angela replied, her voice calm.

"Then I find it difficult to believe that someone as competent as yourself missed a shell corporation running under your nose for that long. Care to explain?"

Angela didn't blink. "I was assigned to payroll and administrative budgeting. I didn't have access to Russell's ledgers or to the town's capital improvement allocations until after his passing."

"Still," Tabitha pressed, "doesn't it strike you as convenient that you discovered it only after his death?"

Angela met her gaze. "It strikes me as unfortunate."

Tabitha arched a brow. "Unfortunate for whom?"

"For the people of Galen Valley. For the taxpayers who trusted their money was being used properly."

Tabitha took a step closer. "Let's talk about the report you submitted to the State Auditor's Office. Are you aware that their office has not publicly confirmed the findings as valid?"

Angela stayed composed. "It's a matter of process. Their reviews take time."

"So we're supposed to take your word for it? A former assistant who conveniently discovers evidence against a man accused of abusing his wife—after his death?"

Angela didn't flinch. "I'm not asking the jury to take my word for anything. I'm asking them to look at the documents."

"And what if those documents were fabricated?"

"Objection," Quentin snapped, standing quickly. "There's been no foundation laid to suggest forgery."

"Sustained," Judge Nelson said sharply. "Ms. Welsh, stay within the bounds."

Tabitha gave a tight nod, then turned back to Angela. "No further questions—*for now.*"

She returned to her seat with clipped strides.

Judge Nelson looked over his glasses. "Does the defense wish to call another witness?"

Quentin stood. "No, Your Honor. The defense rests."

A hush fell over the room.

Judge Nelson looked at the jury. "Ladies and gentlemen, we will recess for the remainder of the afternoon. The state will begin its rebuttal case tomorrow morning at 9 AM. Court is adjourned."

The gavel cracked.

As the crowd began to file out, murmuring and whispering, Natalie stood near the back wall, already tapping furiously into her phone.

Tomorrow would bring the state's last attempt to reclaim the story.

But today?

Today had belonged to the defense.

50

Natalie knocked gently on Cassie's office door and opened it without waiting for a response. Cassie looked up from a stack of budget reports, immediately breaking into a relieved smile at seeing her friend.

"I was hoping you'd stop by," Cassie said, gesturing to the chair across from her desk. "I've been glued to my phone all day, refreshing your blog updates."

Natalie sank into the seat, exhaling deeply. "Today was exhausting. But Angela—Cassie, you would've been so proud. She was incredible up there. Tabitha came at her like she was on trial herself, but Angela didn't flinch."

Cassie leaned back in her chair. "Angela's always been tougher than she looks. And smarter, too."

"Well, she made Tabitha furious," Natalie said with a satisfied smirk. "You could practically see smoke coming out of her ears."

Cassie laughed softly. "Of course she's angry. Tabitha's losing this case, and she knows it."

"Exactly," Natalie agreed. "I think even the jury could sense it."

They sat quietly for a moment, the stress of recent weeks hanging in the silence between them.

Cassie finally broke it. "Since court let out early, what are you planning to do with the rest of your afternoon?"

Natalie smiled wistfully. "I'm going home to take a nap, and then see what Baxter wants to do for dinner. I've earned it today."

"Oh, a nap sounds divine," Cassie sighed. "I used to be able to do that, but not anymore."

Natalie tilted her head thoughtfully. "You know, you don't have to run again. You could make this mayor thing temporary—go back to naps and quiet afternoons."

Cassie chuckled softly, the smile fading as she considered it. "It might be temporary anyway. There's no guarantee I'd win if I run again."

Natalie's eyes softened. "Of course you'd win. Everyone loves you."

"That's sweet," Cassie said gently, "but trust me, not everyone does. I still get notes."

Natalie frowned, leaning forward slightly. "Notes? What kind of notes?"

Cassie hesitated for a moment, then pulled open her desk drawer. She took out a folded sheet of paper, handing it carefully to Natalie.

"Like this one," Cassie said quietly. "I received it not long after I took office."

Natalie unfolded the note, reading silently:

Mayor Dixon,

Congratulations on your new office.

But beware—there is someone within your administration who is not who they appear to be.

Everyone has skeletons in the closet.

Some are just buried deeper than others.

Be prepared, Mayor Dixon. Your office will be in turmoil.

It's coming soon.

Natalie's face paled slightly as she finished reading. "Cassie, when exactly did you get this?"

"Not long after I was sworn in. At the time, I thought it was a prank or just someone stirring up drama after everything we went through with Denise Carrow."

Natalie shook her head slowly. "I don't know, Cass. Re-read this now, knowing everything we do about Russell. Maybe this wasn't just a prank. Maybe someone was trying to warn you."

Cassie took the note back, reading the words again with fresh eyes. A chill ran down her spine. "You might be right."

"You really should've shown this to Baxter," Natalie urged gently. "Maybe he could've helped."

Cassie sighed, folding the paper again and placing it back in her drawer. "I should have, but it's too late now."

Natalie stood up, gathering her purse. "Okay, maybe it's too late for that one. But please promise me, Cass, if you get another note or anything else strange, you'll take it straight to Baxter."

Cassie smiled warmly. "I promise."

Natalie headed toward the door, turning one last time to look back. "Alright, bestie. I'm out of here to enjoy my nap."

Cassie's eyes twinkled playfully. "I'm jealous."

Natalie laughed lightly and slipped out, closing the door gently behind her.

Cassie sat quietly, staring at the closed drawer, the note still echoing through her mind. Her instincts tingled—a feeling she knew too well. She whispered softly to the empty room:

"Skeletons indeed."

51

"If she walks in that door, it'll tell us everything we need to know," Quentin said under his breath as he and his team stepped into the courtroom that morning.

Abigail adjusted her briefcase strap. "You think they'll actually put her on the stand?"

"Oh, I *hope* they do," he replied with a crooked grin. "It'll mean they're cornered—and that their rebuttal is built on desperation, not truth."

Emily, ever cautious, added, "But she's sharp, Quentin. Sandra knows how to spin a narrative."

"I'm counting on it," he replied as he slid into his chair and scanned the room.

And then—there she was.

Sandra Greer, dressed in a slate-gray pencil skirt and cream silk blouse, hair in a tight French twist, heels crisp and conservative. Her expression was neutral, but behind her eyes sat the poise of someone who had been *prepped*.

Quentin glanced across the aisle and saw Tabitha and Paul whispering with purpose, shoulders tense. This wasn't a power play. It was damage control.

Judge Nelson took the bench. "Court is now in session. Ms. Welsh, you may proceed."

Tabitha stood, voice steady.

"The prosecution calls Sandra Greer to the stand."

Gasps fluttered across the gallery. Natalie, already typing from the back of the courtroom, looked up sharply.

Sandra took the stand, sworn in under oath, and sat with her spine ruler-straight.

Tabitha approached with careful grace.

"Ms. Greer, can you tell the court about your professional relationship with Russell Wallen?"

Sandra nodded. "Russell and I worked together for several years. I was Communications Director for Pinecrest County municipal governments. Russell and his team often collaborated with me on budget planning and infrastructure projects so I could relay that information to the public."

"Did your relationship with Mr. Wallen ever become *personal?*"

Sandra drew in a breath, let it out slowly. "Yes. Briefly. A few years ago. It was a mistake, and we both knew it. We ended it quickly."

"Why?"

"Because Russell loved his wife," Sandra said plainly. "He felt guilty, and he ended it. After that, our relationship was strictly professional."

"And did anyone else know about the affair?"

"No," she said. "I did not think so but now I know that Fergus knew about it. I thought we had kept it quiet because it was over before it ever truly began."

Tabitha nodded and paced slowly. "Ms. Greer, did Mr. Wallen ever lay a hand on you in anger? Ever abuse you in any way?"

"No," Sandra said firmly. "The bruises that Mr. Greer mentioned in his testimony—I told him then, and I'll say it again here—they came from a slip in the shower room at a spa in Buckhead. Russell never hurt me."

"And were you aware of any abuse between Russell and Patrice?"

"I never witnessed anything that would indicate abuse," Sandra said. "He rarely even spoke about his home life. But from what I did see, they were cordial—supportive even."

Tabitha returned to her table and picked up a file.

"Let's shift to the financial records that were introduced into evidence. Are you aware of the shell corporations listed in those documents?"

Sandra's expression turned guarded. "Yes."

"Were you involved in the creation of any of them?"

"I signed a few of the documents. At the time, I believed they were for legitimate investment channels Russell was exploring to build reserve funds for infrastructure."

Tabitha narrowed her gaze. "And now?"

Sandra swallowed hard. "Now I believe I was manipulated."

"By whom?" Tabitha asked, her tone still composed.

"By Russell," Sandra said quietly.

That word sent a ripple through the gallery.

Tabitha paused for effect, then stepped closer. "Please explain what you mean by that."

Sandra nodded slowly. "During the brief time we were involved… I was smitten. I trusted him implicitly. He asked me to sign some paperwork—corporate filings, budget projections tied to external infrastructure grants. At the time, I didn't question it. I was thinking with my heart, not my head."

"Do you now regret being involved?"

"Yes," Sandra said firmly. "I know I did wrong. I shouldn't have signed those documents without verifying them. I shouldn't have let my personal feelings cloud my professional judgment."

Tabitha glanced briefly toward the jury, then back to Sandra.

"So let's be clear: Russell Wallen—as charming and professionally competent as he may have been—committed financial fraud. He misled you and others. He deceived the public with taxpayer funds. But with *you*, Sandra—he was kind? Gentle?"

Sandra blinked back the slightest hint of emotion. "Yes. He never laid a hand on me. I would have never feared Russell."

Tabitha gave a single nod. "Thank you. No more questions, Your Honor."

Judge Nelson turned toward the defense table. "Mr. Stiles, your cross?"

Quentin stood slowly, buttoned his jacket, and approached the stand with deliberate calm.

"Ms. Greer, you testified just now that you signed financial documents without truly understanding what they were... is that correct?"

Sandra shifted in her seat. "Yes. I was... emotionally compromised."

"And yet, those documents are now part of a state audit, detailing what appears to be an elaborate laundering scheme involving you, Russell Wallen, and Veronica Altameda."

"Yes."

Quentin picked up a file and glanced at it before continuing. "Are you aware that the State Auditor's Office has turned over preliminary findings to state investigators, and that indictments are likely pending?"

Sandra hesitated.

"I asked if you were aware, Ms. Greer."

"Yes," she finally said. "I am aware."

"So you're facing criminal charges for financial fraud."

Sandra stiffened. "Possibly."

"And in exchange for your cooperation with the prosecution—your willingness to sit here today and paint Russell Wallen as a man who made one mistake in love but was otherwise an altruistic hero—you've been offered a reduced sentence. Maybe even house arrest instead of jail time."

"I didn't lie," Sandra said quickly. "Everything I said was true."

Quentin took a step closer. "But how can we know that? You are testifying under a deal—a motive—to protect yourself. How are we supposed to believe *any* of your testimony when you're testifying to save your own skin?"

"That's not true!" Sandra snapped, her voice rising. "I'm telling you what happened! Russell didn't abuse anyone. He—he was trying to *fix* it!"

"Objection!" Tabitha shouted, springing to her feet. "Your Honor, the defense is badgering the witness."

"Sustained," Judge Nelson said sternly. "Mr. Stiles, reel it in."

Quentin turned away from Sandra, now trembling in the witness chair, and walked back toward his table. Without missing a beat, he said flatly, "No further questions, Your Honor. I'm done with this witness. Can't trust that she's telling the truth anyway—not with the deal she made."

"Objection!" Tabitha shouted again, her voice sharp.

"Sustained!" Judge Nelson barked. "Clerk, strike Counselor's comment from the record. Jury will disregard the last statement made by the defense."

But the damage was done.

The jury had heard it. They'd seen the tremble in Sandra's hands. The flinch in her voice. The desperation behind her composure.

As Sandra stepped down and hurried back to her seat, Quentin leaned toward Abigail and whispered, "They just handed us reasonable doubt—gift-wrapped."

And from the back of the courtroom, Natalie already knew what her next headline would be.

52

Title: **In a Surprise Move, the State Makes Its Final Plea**
Posted at 10:17 a.m.

Well, readers—this morning brought something we weren't expecting.

At exactly 9:00 a.m., with the courtroom packed and the defense team still settling into their seats, District Attorney Tabitha Welsh stood and informed Judge Nelson that the state was ready to proceed with closing arguments.

Even Quentin Stiles appeared taken aback. He had his team huddled and legal pads in hand, clearly still preparing for what they thought would be a continuation of rebuttal testimony.

Judge Nelson simply nodded and said, "Very well, Counselors. Proceed."

And with that, the state began its final effort to convince the jury that Patrice Wallen should be found guilty—not just of murder, but of premeditated murder worthy of the death penalty.

The first to speak was Assistant District Attorney Paul Barnes. True to his reputation, his delivery was methodical, emotionless, almost surgical.

He walked the jury step by step through the morning of the shooting:

- The hike on Wren Hollow Trail, allegedly for Russell's health.

- The gunshot, and the Ellis siblings who heard it and discovered Patrice standing over Russell's body, gun in hand.

- The 911 call, the paramedics, the lack of any attempt to flee.

He reminded the jury that Patrice admitted to shooting her husband, that there was no struggle visible on his body, and that the gunshot was clean and fatal.

Then Tabitha Welsh took the floor, and her tone was far less clinical.

She leaned hard into the absence of corroborated abuse:

- The only documented ER visit never resulted in charges or even an official domestic violence report.

- Patrice's coworkers, women who saw her daily, testified to never seeing bruises or emotional distress.

- Her own mother said she never suspected anything was wrong.

And then, as expected, Tabitha drove home the point the state has been building toward since the insurance bombshell dropped:

"The jury must consider the life insurance policy, taken out just three weeks before the shooting," she said.

"Patrice Wallen had motive, opportunity, and a plan. She lured her husband into the woods, ensured they were alone, and then shot him. That is not impulse. That is premeditation."

Her voice grew sharper as she paced in front of the jury box.

"People have affairs. People make financial mistakes. But they don't all end up shot dead on a hiking trail by their spouse. This was not self-defense. This was cold calculation—and it deserves the maximum punishment our state allows: death."

A hush fell across the courtroom when she said it.

No theatrics. No raised voices. Just two seasoned prosecutors laying down their version of the truth.

Whether the jury will buy it is another matter entirely.

But one thing is clear: The gloves are off.

Stay tuned. Quentin Stiles will have his turn tomorrow—and if his track record tells us anything, it's that his closing argument may just be the most powerful moment of this entire trial.

I'll be there.

You should be too.

— Natalie

The low hum of evening traffic passed outside the boutique's display windows, but inside, the small sitting area near the back was alive with chatter and clinking teacups.

Cassie Dixon sat curled in one of the velvet chairs, a steaming mug of chai in hand. Across from her, Kathryn had kicked off her heels and tucked her legs beneath her on the settee. Margaret, always composed, sat upright on the arm of the loveseat. Natalie perched at the edge of the coffee table, animated and wide-eyed.

"I'm still not over how fast that happened," Cassie said, shaking her head. "I thought they'd drag out rebuttal testimony for at least another day or two."

"I think it means they know Sandra didn't land the save they were counting on," Margaret said, crossing her arms. "The woman looked like she'd rehearsed that story in a mirror every night for a week. And she still couldn't keep the emotion straight."

"They gambled and lost," Kathryn added. "Sandra was a Hail Mary, and she dropped the ball. Quentin dismantled her."

Natalie leaned in, voice hushed like they were sharing secrets. "I still can't believe Tabitha tried to end strong with that life insurance argument. She said 'death' like she was casting a curse."

Cassie sighed. "I hate that word. I hate that it's even on the table."

"Well," Margaret said, sipping her tea, "the jury's job is to look at facts, not feelings. But I'll be honest—*I* don't think they're going to give the death penalty. Not with what Angela uncovered. Not with the abuse allegations, the financial scandal, the affair. It's all just... too messy."

Natalie nodded slowly. "I agree. I think the jury will find her not guilty of first-degree murder, maybe guilty of a lesser charge. Manslaughter, possibly. Or maybe not guilty at all."

"Same," said Kathryn. "Especially after Lorinda testified. That shook people. You could *feel* it in the courtroom."

Cassie tapped her mug against her lip. "I don't know. Juries are unpredictable. I just hope... whatever they decide, it brings some peace. To everyone."

Natalie glanced at the clock. "You know what's wild? Tomorrow could be it. This time tomorrow, we could be waiting on a verdict."

Margaret looked toward the window, her expression thoughtful. "Or watching a town try to rebuild itself after hearing one."

53

The courtroom was quiet. Not just the kind of silence that came with respect, but the tense, aching stillness that blanketed a space before something big—something final.

The jury sat in place. Natalie, seated five rows back per usual, had already positioned her laptop to capture every word. Baxter stood along the back wall beside Seth, arms folded.

Judge Nelson gave a slight nod.

"Defense, you may proceed."

Quentin Stiles rose, one hand smoothing the front of his suit. He didn't walk to the center of the courtroom with fanfare. He moved slowly, methodically—like a man carrying the weight of another person's life in his hands.

"Good morning," he began, turning toward the jury with a soft, level tone. "You've heard a lot over the past several weeks. You've seen exhibits, heard from experts, from eyewitnesses, from friends and family—people on both sides trying to tell you what they believe to be the truth."

He paused, letting the silence stretch.

"I want to take you back to the testimony that I believe tells you everything you need to know. Lorinda Beaumont, a respected ER nurse, someone with no agenda, no stake in this case—took that witness stand and told you about the night Patrice Wallen came into the emergency room."

He stepped toward the jury box, voice quiet but firm.

"She testified that Patrice's injuries were severe. That her face was bruised—beyond what makeup could conceal. That she begged

Patrice to report the abuse. She and Dr. Clay Moreau both did. That's not the story of a woman capable of plotting murder. That's the story of a woman who was terrified... and didn't yet have the courage to act."

He walked a few paces, hands now gesturing slightly.

"Now, the prosecution wants you to focus on what *wasn't* seen. On the co-workers who didn't notice bruises. On the mother who didn't suspect abuse. But let me ask you—how many victims of domestic violence go unseen? How many suffer in silence? It's not about what was visible. It's about what was endured."

Quentin turned toward the front row where Patrice sat, her head bowed, fingers trembling slightly in her lap.

"She kept a journal. A private one. Not a manifesto, not a plan. Just the thoughts of a woman trying to survive her reality. The state used those pages to try to convince you of premeditation. But I ask you—isn't it more likely those entries reflect fear? Guilt? Maybe even the desperate hope for change?"

He turned back to the jury, voice rising with conviction.

"Patrice didn't flee that trail. She didn't toss the gun into the woods and vanish. She laid it down. She curled into a fetal position and cried. She cooperated fully with law enforcement."

He let that sink in before moving forward.

"And let's talk about the life insurance policy. You remember Irene Hopkins, the insurance agent. She said that yes, Patrice initiated the process. But her assistant spoke with Russell directly—about issues with the e-signature process. So let me ask you—does that sound like a wife plotting murder? Or a couple having a normal conversation about financial planning after a doctor's recommendation to take health more seriously?"

He stopped in front of the jury box.

"And wasn't it Patrice who urged Russell to go on that hike? To get fresh air, improve his health? She didn't lure him out there with malice. She wanted him to get better. She wanted to walk beside him as he did."

He lowered his voice.

"What happened on that trail wasn't premeditated. It was a scuffle. A moment of fear. She tried to take the gun from him, and it went off. One second… that's all it took. And now he's gone. And she's on trial for her life."

The jury was listening now, motionless.

"Ladies and gentlemen, when you go into that deliberation room, I ask you to do one thing: Consider the facts. Not emotion. Not the noise. The facts."

He stepped back slightly, his voice firm.

"There is reasonable doubt. There is more than enough evidence to believe that Patrice Wallen acted in self-defense. That she tried to save herself from a man who had, by all accounts, controlled and frightened her for years. There is no ironclad proof that this was murder—only tragedy."

He took one final pause.

"And that is what I ask of you. Don't let this tragedy become another one. Don't send a woman to death row for defending herself. Don't tell victims of abuse that they must die in silence or be punished for surviving."

He looked each juror in the eye, one by one.

"If you believe—even for one second—that this was anything but a tragic accident in the midst of abuse, you must return a verdict of not guilty."

He walked slowly back to the defense table, placing both hands on the polished wood surface.

"Thank you for your service. And thank you for listening."

He sat.

Silence.

Judge Nelson cleared his throat, looking toward the jury.

"We will recess for one hour. When we return, I will issue your instructions and send you into deliberation."

The gavel echoed through the courtroom.

And as Natalie finished typing the last few lines of her blog post, she whispered to herself, "Now we wait."

54

The scent of grilling steaks wafted through the air as the sun dipped low over Galen Valley. The backyard of the Dixon home had become something of a sanctuary over the past several weeks—a place where friends could decompress, surrounded by good food, familiar voices, and just enough distance from the courtroom.

Baxter stood at the grill, flipping thick cuts of ribeye while nursing a bottle of craft beer. Seth was beside him, tongs in hand, watching the flames flare up.

"I swear," Seth said, "the courthouse feels like a war zone. Today was intense."

Baxter grunted. "It's not over yet. Jury's probably just settling in. They've got a lot to chew through."

"Not as much as we do," Seth replied, nodding toward the platter of steaks.

Behind them, Cassie, Kathryn, and Natalie were relaxing on the back porch, each with a glass of wine. Brontë, ever the quiet one, sat in the corner chair with a sweet tea in hand and his signature flannel sleeves rolled up.

Cassie exhaled slowly, eyes trained on the darkening sky. "I still can't believe it ended so quickly. I thought for sure they'd spend another day on testimony."

"Quentin didn't need another day," Natalie said. "He landed every point this morning. It was quiet in the courtroom, like everyone was holding their breath."

Kathryn took a sip of her wine. "The question is, how long before the jury comes to a decision? Are we looking at a few hours or a few days?"

"Hard to say," Baxter called from the grill. "Depends on how dead-locked they get. And judging by the mood out there, it's going to be a tug-of-war."

Natalie unlocked her phone and refreshed her blog page. "You want proof of that? Just look at my comments section."

"Oh no," Cassie said with a smirk. "We're doing that tonight?"

"Absolutely," Natalie replied. "It's like a psychological study—half the town and people beyond are screaming 'GUILTY,' and the other half think she should be walking out a free woman tomorrow morning."

"Read us a few," Kathryn said, settling back.

Natalie cleared her throat theatrically and began scrolling.

@JusticeFirst89: "Patrice lured him out there. That insurance policy says it all. She had a plan, and she executed it. Plain and simple."

"Classic prosecution echo," Natalie muttered. "And here's another one…"

@HopefulHeart: "I was in an abusive marriage for ten years. You learn how to hide the bruises. You learn how to smile through it. Patrice is me, and I pray she walks free."

The mood on the porch shifted.

"Damn," said Cassie, eyes softening. "That one hit me."

Natalie nodded. "That comment has over two hundred likes already."

"Keep going," Brontë said quietly. "Let's hear more."

Natalie scrolled.

@GalValleyNative: "I worked at the courthouse for three years. Never saw anything strange with Russell. Patrice was cold, distant. Doesn't mean she's guilty, but I'm not buying the victim act."

@TruthTeller87: "It's not about what you see—it's what's hidden. People like Russell know how to control the narrative. Just because no one saw it doesn't mean it didn't happen."

Kathryn leaned over to glance at Natalie's screen. "Your readers are split right down the middle."

"They are," Natalie said, refreshing again. "Dozens more comments just came in since I sat down. Look at this one..."

@RedFlagMom: "I had a patient once come into the ER like Patrice. Said she fell down stairs. Her injuries said otherwise. The system failed her. I hope the system doesn't fail Patrice."

@NoExcuseForMurder: "If she was abused, she should've left. Not killed him. People are twisting abuse to excuse murder. That's not okay."

Natalie looked up from the screen. "It's honestly jarring to see how polarizing this is. And most of these people are basing their opinions on the blog and the trial coverage. Not even sitting in the courtroom."

"People see what they want to see," Baxter said, carrying over the platter of grilled steaks. "And they bring their own experiences with them. That jury's doing the same thing right now."

They all moved to the picnic table where plates were being passed, silverware clinked against ceramic, and the soft chirp of crickets filled in the background between sips of wine and conversation.

"So what do we think?" Seth asked as he carved into his steak. "Real talk—what's your prediction?"

"Not guilty," Natalie said without hesitation. "Too much reasonable doubt. And I think Angela and Lorinda were powerful witnesses."

"I agree," said Cassie. "The jury may not like the insurance policy, but the timeline's murky enough to cast doubt on motive."

Baxter chewed thoughtfully before answering. "I don't think they'll acquit her completely. My gut says manslaughter. They'll find her guilty of something, but not first-degree murder. And definitely not the death penalty."

Brontë nodded. "That feels about right."

Kathryn twirled her fork in her mashed potatoes. "I still think there's a chance she walks. And if she does, Joyce Conrad is going to lose it."

"She already has," said Natalie. "Did you see how she reacted to Angela and Fergus?"

"Lord, yes," Kathryn said with a shake of her head. "Baxter, you should've cuffed her on the spot for contempt."

Baxter chuckled. "She's been warned. Next time, she's out."

They all laughed softly, but the weight of the conversation lingered.

As the evening wore on, the moon began to rise, and the backyard lights cast a golden glow over the table.

Natalie refreshed her blog one more time and read aloud one last comment:

@BetweenTheLines: "This case is more than a murder trial. It's a reflection of how we treat victims, how we process secrets, and how we assign guilt. No matter the verdict, something in this town has shifted."

Everyone went quiet for a moment.

"Well," said Cassie, voice low, "they're not wrong."

"I think we're all a little different than we were when this started," Seth added.

Brontë stood and stretched. "Reckon we better clean up before we get philosophical."

"Too late," Kathryn said with a wink.

They all chuckled as they began gathering plates and rinsing glasses, moving through the motions of normalcy as the jury—somewhere, just a few miles away—sat in deliberation.

And in that pocket of peace with stars dotting the night sky, six people found comfort in each other's presence. Whatever the verdict, whatever came next.

<h1 style="text-align:center">55</h1>

The blinds in the District Attorney's office were partially drawn, streaks of gray light cutting across the room like slashes. Tabitha sat at her desk, eyes fixed on a half-drunk mug of coffee that had long gone cold. Across from her, Paul leaned back in the visitor's chair, his arms crossed and his jaw tight.

"Two days," Tabitha muttered. "Two whole days."

Paul didn't respond right away. He tapped his pen against the armrest, then finally said, "If it were going our way, we'd know by now."

Tabitha lifted her gaze. "You think?"

He nodded. "Juries don't deliberate this long on clear-cut cases. If they believed our story—about the insurance, the lack of visible abuse, the motive—they'd be done already."

Tabitha leaned back, letting her head hit the leather cushion behind her. "The Conrads are going to hang us out to dry if this comes back not guilty. Joyce has already made it personal. She expected a conviction—and a death sentence."

Paul gave a cynical huff. "She expected blood."

The silence stretched between them.

"What do you think she'll do?" Tabitha asked.

"If we lose?" Paul shrugged. "Public statement, threats of legal action against the state. She'll probably pull favors to damage us politically. She's got connections across the state bar. Judges. Senators."

Tabitha's voice grew quieter. "Do you think it was a mistake—calling Sandra Greer?"

Paul didn't answer for a moment, then finally said, "We were out of options. And you know what? It might have been our only real shot."

Tabitha stared at the jury verdict board on the wall, still blank, and said nothing.

At Galen Valley Town Hall, the conference room buzzed with the sounds of sorting, stapling, and light conversation. Cassie, Angela and Darlene sat around the long table preparing the agenda and budget packets for the upcoming council meeting. A stack of coffee-stained folders sat at the center, slowly diminishing as they worked.

Angela flipped through a printout. "I swear, I've read this same infrastructure funding report five times. I still can't remember if we approved the sidewalk expansion near the elementary school."

"We did," Cassie said, passing her a fresh copy. "Page six."

Darlene smiled faintly. "Good to know some things are still predictable."

Cassie reached for another packet, then paused. "How long do you think it's going to take them?"

"The jury?" Angela asked.

Cassie nodded.

Angela shrugged. "I was sure we'd hear something yesterday. But now… I'm not sure what to think. Every hour that goes by feels heavier."

"I'm guessing they're split," Darlene said, her tone low. "That's the only reason it would be taking this long. Someone's not budging."

"I just hope it's not a hung jury," Angela murmured. "No one deserves to go through all this again."

Cassie stared at the stacks of papers before her, her hands still. "It's strange. After everything we've learned… about Russell, the shell corporations, the affair—I still remember how dedicated he was when we first started rebuilding the town. That version of him… that's the man I thought I knew."

Angela placed a hand over hers. "Sometimes we only see the part they want us to see."

Cassie nodded, then turned back to her packets. "Let's finish these before the verdict comes in. I want everything off my desk before the next storm starts."

At the downtown office of Quentin Stiles, the atmosphere was calm—but taut. Quentin sat at the end of the polished conference table, his phone lying face-up in front of him, the ringer set to maximum volume.

Every few seconds, he glanced down at it, then back up at his team.

Emily was pacing lightly along the bookshelves, one finger tapping the edge of a notepad she hadn't written on in an hour. Abigail had just returned from the detention center and was rubbing her temples as she sat across from Quentin.

"She's calm," Abigail said finally. "I mean, as calm as she can be. She asked me if we'll know today."

"What did you tell her?" Quentin asked.

"That I hoped so. And that if we did, we pray it's in her favor."

Emily glanced toward the phone. "It's been almost forty-eight hours."

Quentin nodded. "And if I had to guess, they've been going back and forth. But the longer this goes, the more I think they're working their way to an agreement."

"You think they're close?" Abigail asked.

"I do. They're tired. They're frustrated. They want to go home."

Emily was about to speak again when the phone rang.

All three jumped.

Quentin grabbed it instantly. "Stiles."

He paused, listening. Then his jaw tightened.

"Yes, thank you. We'll be there in fifteen."

He hung up and looked at Abigail and Emily.

"That was the clerk. The jury's reached a verdict. We have forty-five minutes."

No one spoke for a moment—just long enough for the gravity to settle in.

Then Quentin stood. "Let's go."

Abigail grabbed her briefcase. Emily was already at the door.

56

The gavel fell with a sharp crack.

"All rise," the bailiff intoned.

Judge Robert Nelson entered the courtroom with his usual stoic demeanor, but today, the tension hanging in the air seemed to even stiffen his posture. He took his seat, then nodded to the clerk.

"Bring in the jury."

Natalie was already typing. Her blog post was live, her fingers poised to capture every second as it unfolded.

9:02 AM – The jury has entered the courtroom. After two full days of deliberation, we are moments from hearing the verdict in the State of North Carolina vs. Patrice Valeria Austin Wallen.

The twelve jurors filed in slowly, solemnly, their expressions unreadable. Natalie studied their faces one by one, hoping to catch a flicker of emotion—a tight jaw, a teary glance, anything.

But they didn't look at the defense table. They didn't glance at Tabitha or Paul either.

They just took their seats, facing the bench, their expressions guarded and heavy with duty.

Judge Nelson adjusted his glasses and folded his hands.

"Ladies and gentlemen of the jury," he said, "have you reached a verdict?"

The foreperson, a man in his early sixties with steady eyes and a deeply creased brow, stood and nodded.

"We have, Your Honor."

"Please hand the verdict to the bailiff."

A uniformed officer stepped forward, collected the folded paper, and handed it to the judge. Nelson opened it, eyes scanning the text. He gave no reaction. No twitch of the brow. No crease in his lips. He simply folded it shut again and looked out over the courtroom.

"I remind everyone present that this courtroom is a place of order and respect. There will be no outbursts. I expect full decorum."

Natalie glanced around.

Joyce Conrad sits in the front row, rigid and silent, her husband's hand gripping hers like a tether. Her eyes are locked on the judge, jaw clenched so tightly it's a wonder she doesn't crack a tooth. The defense table is equally still—Patrice Wallen sitting, flanked by Quentin Stiles and Abigail Wentworth. Abigail holds her client's hand, her other arm resting protectively behind Patrice's back. Quentin's eyes never leave the judge. Emily Jacobs looks behind her—briefly—at Patrice's mother, Valerie Austin, who sits with her head down, shoulders shaking in silent sobs.

The silence grew.

Even the breath in the room seemed to pause.

"Will the defendant please rise."

Quentin and Abigail both stood with Patrice, steadying her as her knees threatened to give way.

"Foreperson," the judge said. "Please read the verdict aloud."

The man stood again, unfolded a second slip of paper, and in a voice neither proud nor apologetic, simply read:

"We the jury find the defendant, Patrice Valeria Austin Wallen, not guilty."

A hush swept the room.

No gasps. No shouts. Just the sound of Patrice's knees buckling as she collapsed into her chair, sobbing into Abigail's shoulder.

Natalie's fingers flew.

9:08 AM – Not guilty. It's official. The courtroom is stunned into silence. Patrice Wallen has been acquitted of all charges in the death of her husband, Russell Wallen.

Patrice has collapsed in tears, unable to stand on her own. Abigail is holding her, whispering something in her ear. Quentin stands stone-faced but his eyes are glassy. Emily has turned again to Valerie, who is openly weeping now, hands covering her mouth.

From the prosecution table, Joyce Conrad began to rise, rage flashing in her eyes—but her husband pulled her back down with surprising strength.

Tabitha, sensing what was coming, turned and held up a hand, signaling for patience, for control. Joyce shook her head, her mouth forming words—but she didn't speak them aloud.

"Your Honor," Tabitha said, standing. "The prosecution requests the jury be polled."

Judge Nelson nodded once. "So ordered."

He turned back to the jury.

"I will now ask each of you to state your verdict aloud. Juror One—how do you find?"

"Not guilty."

"Juror Two?"

"Not guilty."

"Juror Three?"

"Not guilty."

On it went—each of the twelve repeating the words that struck like thunder to one half of the courtroom, and salvation to the other.

Natalie's blog post:

9:12 AM – The jury has been polled. All twelve have confirmed the verdict: not guilty. Patrice Wallen will walk free.

Natalie looked up from her laptop and toward the back wall of the courtroom. Baxter was standing beside Seth, both of them wearing quiet smiles, their eyes fixed on Patrice.

Seth exhaled a long, slow breath. Baxter gave a single, subtle nod.

It was over.

Not with a bang, not with chaos—but with a quiet, searing exhale of justice finally catching up with truth.

And outside those walls, Galen Valley would never be the same again.

57

The moment the courthouse doors opened, the air erupted with sound.

Cameras flashed. Microphones jutted forward. Reporters, both local and regional, surged toward the steps like a tidal wave crashing onto dry land.

Tabitha and Paul descended the marble stairs first, flanking Joyce and Lawrence in a four-person wall of tension.

Joyce, wrapped in a severe black coat and large sunglasses, looked like she'd stepped out of a political scandal. She clutched her husband's arm with a grip that looked more like possession than support.

"Mrs. Conrad, do you believe justice was served?"

"What will your family do next?"

"Are you considering a civil case against Patrice Wallen?"

Joyce ripped off her sunglasses and snapped at the nearest camera. "Justice was not served! That woman killed my son in cold blood. And now she walks free? We will not rest until real justice is done."

Lawrence gently tried to pull her back, but she was already in full force.

"She manipulated everyone! Don't talk to me about due process when the facts were twisted and the real victim is dead."

Behind her, Tabitha kept her expression measured. Her eyes swept the crowd before stepping forward to the mics.

"We're disappointed," she said calmly. "But we respect the jury's decision. That's the foundation of our legal system—even when we disagree with the outcome."

Paul nodded beside her. "We presented the case to the best of our ability. The jury weighed it carefully. We'll review everything and decide how to move forward from here."

Joyce opened her mouth again, but this time, Lawrence took her firmly by the arm and pulled her aside. Reporters called after them, their questions rising into a chaotic din.

Around the corner of the building, where the cameras hadn't dared to follow, Quentin, Abigail and Emily emerged from a side exit with Patrice and her mother, Valerie.

Patrice was still trembling, her eyes swollen and red, her mouth unable to form full sentences yet.

"Come on," Quentin said gently, placing a guiding hand on her back.

They moved quickly, heads low, crossing the alley and climbing into Quentin's black sedan. Abigail slid in behind them, still holding Patrice's hand.

Valerie climbed in last, her voice barely above a whisper. "Thank you for everything."

Quentin simply nodded, pulled the door closed, and turned on the ignition.

As they drove away in silence, the chaos of the courthouse fell away behind them.

Meanwhile, Natalie, Baxter, and Seth exited through the front, blending into the onlookers gathered near the sidewalk. The buzz of live cameras and amplified voices made conversation impossible at first, so they stood side-by-side, watching.

Natalie was still typing on her phone, updating her blog post in real-time.

10:02 AM – The scene outside the courthouse is equal parts pandemonium and grief. Joyce Conrad made a fiery statement denouncing the ver-

dict. The prosecution remained professional and composed. Meanwhile, the defense wisely avoided the spotlight, leaving through a side exit.

This case may be legally over, but the court of public opinion is just getting started.

As she typed, a local news crew swung their camera toward a group of high school seniors holding handmade signs that read *Justice for Patrice* and *Believe Victims*. Across the street, another group shouted at them about murder and accountability.

Natalie sighed. "This is going to ripple for a long time."

"No doubt," Seth said, glancing at his watch. "I've got about ten voicemails already. Everyone wants to talk."

Baxter chuckled. "Let's hope none of them are the mayor."

"I wouldn't bet on it," Seth said with a half-smile. "But I'm heading to my truck. I need air."

He started walking, then turned back.

"I'm sure Cassie'll want us all to get together," he said over his shoulder.

Baxter nodded. "Just text us when."

Natalie watched Seth walk off, then turned to Baxter. "Let's get out of here too. This circus isn't going anywhere."

He held the cruiser door open for her. "Agreed. You did good, Nat. Your coverage—your heart—it's been something special."

She smiled, touched. "Thanks. Let's go home."

They pulled out onto the street as the courthouse grew smaller in the rearview mirror. The crowd was still shouting, the reporters still filming.

But for now—for this moment—it was over.

58

It was a soft evening in Galen Valley, the kind of night that felt like a quiet exhale after months of holding breath. The boutique windows at Valley Vogue glowed golden beneath the street lamps. Inside, jazz played low through the speakers, and the scent of citrus candles mingled with the subtle aroma of merlot.

Cassie, Natalie, Kathryn, and Margaret sat on tufted chairs arranged around a low table near the front of the store. Their wine glasses sparkled in the light, half-full and gleaming with red warmth. It had been several weeks since the verdict, and the evening was the first time they had all truly exhaled together.

"I still think about it," Natalie said, brushing her fingers along the rim of her glass. "The silence in that courtroom after the verdict. Like the whole world paused to recalibrate."

"Not just the world," Margaret said. "This town too. People have changed. Eyes have been opened."

"I think that's what justice really is," Cassie added. "Not just a verdict—but what we do after it."

"I'll toast to that," Kathryn said, raising her glass.

Before they could clink glasses, a knock echoed through the boutique.

They all turned.

"I'll get it," Cassie said, setting her glass down and walking to the door. She unlocked it and opened it slowly.

Standing there, hand-in-hand, were Patrice Wallen and Valerie Austin.

For a heartbeat, no one moved.

Then Cassie broke into a warm smile. "Well, this is a surprise."

"May we come in?" Patrice asked softly. "Just for a moment."

"Of course," Cassie said, stepping aside.

The women entered, and the room seemed to still with reverence.

"I didn't mean to intrude on your evening," Patrice said, eyes sweeping the familiar faces, "but we wanted to come... to say thank you."

Valerie smiled, her expression one of quiet pride. "Truly. From the bottom of our hearts."

"You don't owe us thanks," Margaret said, standing.

"Oh, but we do," Patrice insisted. "We used the donations, your generous donations and some of our own savings, and... we purchased a large old bed and breakfast in Asheville."

Natalie straightened in her seat, eyes widening.

"We've turned it into a women's shelter," Valerie said. "We live on the top floor. The other two floors are for women—any woman—who needs a place to feel safe. Who needs time to breathe. To start over."

Tears shimmered in Patrice's eyes.

"We could never have done it without you all. And your readers, Natalie. I get dozens of letters and donations every single day because of your blog. Even more important, it's reaching women. Real women. They're finding us. They're showing up on our doorstep."

Natalie's hand covered her mouth, overcome.

"When I ask how they found out about our shelter," Patrice continued, "most of them say your name. Your blog. Your words." She crossed the room and pulled Natalie into a hug. "You gave me my voice back. And now you're giving it to others too."

Kathryn blinked back tears. "We are so pleased to help. And we want to do even more."

"Come visit us," Patrice said, looking at all four women. "Come often. We'd love to have you. We've got big plans—a community garden, art therapy workshops, and one day maybe even transitional housing. But just having you walk through the door... it tells the women who stay there that they matter. That someone sees them."

Margaret reached for her wine and raised it toward Patrice and Valerie. "To rising from the ashes. And to helping others fly."

Cassie nodded. "We support you one hundred percent, Patrice."

Patrice's eyes shone as she stepped back toward the door with her mother. "Thank you. That means more than I can ever say. To me... and to the women who come through those doors. Just knowing someone cares... that's all it takes to start over."

She smiled one last time.

And then the door closed softly behind them, leaving the four women inside surrounded by the warm hum of the boutique, hearts fuller than when the evening began.

Author's Note

This story may be fictional, but the truths it reflects are very real.

Every day, countless individuals—most often women—suffer from domestic abuse in silence. They endure fear, manipulation, and violence behind closed doors, often without support or a safe place to turn. Many, like Patrice in this story, hide their pain, convinced they must bear it alone or fearful that no one will believe them.

But no one should suffer in silence.

If this book has touched you, I urge you to take that emotion and channel it into action. Reach out to a local women's shelter or domestic violence resource center in your community. Support them with your time, your donations, your voice. Even the smallest gesture—like donating gently used clothing, toiletries, or a warm meal—can make a world of difference in someone's journey to safety and healing.

And if you or someone you know is in an abusive situation, please know: **you are not alone**. There is help. There is hope. There are people who care deeply and who will stand with you every step of the way.

Let's build a world where no one has to hide their bruises behind smiles or stay silent out of fear. Together, we can shine light into the shadows.

With love and solidarity,

LG Rice

Website: www.authorlgrice.com   Email: hello@authorlgrice.com

RESOURCES

If you or someone you love is experiencing domestic abuse, please know that help is available. You are not alone.

Here are some national resources in the United States that provide free, confidential support 24/7:

National Domestic Violence Hotline

1-800-799-SAFE (7233)
Text "START" to **88788**
www.thehotline.org
Live chat available on website
Provides support, safety planning, and local shelter connections.

National Sexual Assault Hotline (RAINN)

1-800-656-HOPE (4673)
www.rainn.org
Offers anonymous support and connects survivors to local service providers.

StrongHearts Native Helpline (for Native American and Alaska Native communities)

1-844-7NATIVE (1-844-762-8483)
www.strongheartshelpline.org
Culturally-appropriate, confidential support for Native peoples.

Love Is Respect (for teens and young adults)

1-866-331-9474
Text "LOVEIS" to **22522**
www.loveisrespect.org
Dedicated to empowering youth to identify and prevent dating abuse.

Support Local Shelters

To find a local women's shelter or domestic violence organization in your area, visit: www.domesticshelters.org

You can search by zip code to find shelters, counseling, legal aid, and support groups near you.

Together, we can make a difference. Thank you for caring, for reading, and for being part of the movement to help survivors find safety, healing, and hope.

www.ingramcontent.com/pod-product-compliance
Lightning Source LLC
Chambersburg PA
CBHW070554120726
47909CB00007B/2336